ROMANCING DR. LOVE

BOOK ONE

REBECCA HEFLIN

ACKNOWLEDGMENTS

To my ever-faithful beta readers, Yvonne and my hubby, Ron. Thank you for your continued guidance, patience, and support.

And to my editor, Paul, your keen eye and indepth knowledge of all things grammarly are much appreciated. Your skill allows my stories to shine.

"How on earth are you ever going to explain in terms of chemistry and physics so important a biological phenomenon as first love?"

— Albert Einstein

1

"No, no, no. This isn't happening. This isn't happening," Samantha Love muttered as she gently banged her head against the steering wheel.

She turned the key again. Nothing. Not even a wheeze. This was the icing on the cake of her otherwise craptastic day.

A bead of sweat trickled down her back. And another one between her girls. God, she hated boob sweat.

When she'd taken the research and teaching position at Sterling University in North Georgia last fall, she'd never have guessed the summer would be so hot.

Throwing open the door of her car to let in even more stifling heat, she searched for the lever to pop the hood. Finally locating it, she pulled it, then walked around to the front of the car. As if she knew what to do.

Just as she leaned under the hood to jiggle some wire thingies, she heard, "Dr. Love? Do you need some help?"

She let out a startled squeak hitting her head on the

underside of the hood. "Ow!" Rubbing the offended spot, she turned and saw Ethan Quinn standing there looking all adorable. Not to mention manly.

Dammit. Why did it have to be him? "No. I'm fine." Yeah, right. For all her parents' preaching on women and self-sufficiency, she didn't know a dipstick from a spark plug when it came to cars. She turned back to the mystery parts under the hood.

"You need a jump."

"I beg your pardon?" She spun, hand on her hip.

"Your battery." He pointed in the direction of her open hood. "It probably needs a jump."

"Oh. Right." Of course he meant her battery. What else would he be talking about?

"I have jumper cables in my car. I'll have you going in a few minutes."

"He'll have me going in a few minutes," she mumbled under her breath as she watched him walk to the far corner of the parking lot. Tall, athletic build, dark-wash jeans, white button-down shirt. And that hair. Tousled espresso-brown waves just brushing the top of his collar. "He's already got me going," she said to herself.

He tossed his messenger bag in the car and climbed in. And, of course, *his* car started. Because that's what cars did. They started when you turned the key. Then they blew cold air, so you didn't have to stand in the mid-July Georgia heat. Unless they dated back to the Stone Age like hers. Another bead of sweat trickled between her breasts.

She released a wistful sigh. Bet the AC felt good.

He pulled his recent model American-made car around to face hers and then got out to pop the hood. Walking around to the trunk, he opened it and grabbed a set of jumper cables, looking like he knew what he was doing.

Good thing somebody around here did.

"It's a hot one today," Ethan commented, as he connected one of the clamp doohickeys to what she assumed was the car battery. His sleeves were rolled up over his forearms, displaying muscles with a light dusting of hair.

Clamping the other end of the cables to his own battery, he then returned to her car. When he walked past her, his cologne wafted to her nose, temporarily erasing her angst at being in his presence.

Then he touched his hand to her back. And the anxiety returned tenfold. "Stand clear." He leaned into the gaping mouth of the car and attached the remaining clamp, throwing a spark.

"All right. Let's see if we can get this baby going." He climbed into the driver's seat of his car and turned it on.

"Give her a try," he hollered over the din of his car's running motor.

Sam dropped into the front seat and turned the key. The older-than-dirt engine tried but couldn't work up enough energy to turn over.

"Hold on," Ethan called, then revved his car. "Okay, try her again."

Her car wheezed then reluctantly cranked a couple of times before coming to life.

Ethan was at her door, leaning over, hands braced on the roof. "Great. Let her run a bit, then I'll disconnect the cables." A bead of sweat trickled down his temple. "My AC's on full blast. Why don't you sit in my car until yours is ready to go." He stepped aside to give her room to get out.

Sam felt as wilted as week-old lettuce, so against her better judgment she took him up on the offer.

He opened the front passenger door of his shiny black Lincoln MKS—such a gentleman—and she sank into the leather seats and stuck her face in front of the vent. God, it felt good. The door closed with a solid *thunk*. Resisting the urge to wipe away the boob sweat, she settled for drying the perspiration on her face and neck.

The car dipped as Ethan took a seat on the driver's side before shutting the door and closing out the rest of the world. Music played softly in the background—something popular. The intimacy of being alone in the car with Ethan washed over her.

"I'd offer you something cool to drink, but I don't have anything."

She realized she hadn't said a word in the last five minutes. "Thank you."

"No thanks necessary. You'd do the same for me."

"No, I wouldn't." She smiled. "I don't know a thing about cars."

He nodded as a grin split his face. "Well, from the looks of your battery, you're going to need a new one. I can follow you to Burt's Automotive. He can have a replacement installed in fifteen minutes."

She shook her head. "Thanks, but I don't want to put you out in any further."

"It's no trouble. Besides, if you go straight home, I don't think she's going to start for you in the morning."

"Oh." That would not be good.

"She should be juiced up enough to get you to Burt's. Stay here until I unhook the cables." Ethan got out of the car and set to work.

She'd steered clear of Ethan Quinn since the day she was introduced to the rest of the college faculty. The moment they shook hands she'd felt a connection. And from the look on his face, he'd felt it too. That flood of adrenaline, dopamine, and serotonin one feels when there is a strong physical attraction.

Relationships were complicated, but getting situated at a new university was already complicated enough.

No. Being in close proximity to Ethan Quinn was a bad idea. So as much as she hated to leave the cool comfort of his car, she jumped out and got in her rolling oven before he could say otherwise.

HIS LUCKY DAY, Ethan thought. Burt's was a little backed up, so they were looking at a turn-around time of half an hour to forty-five minutes.

"How about a cold drink over at Ruby's?" he indicated the town diner across the street.

"You don't have to wait with me."

"My father always taught me never to leave a woman in distress."

She laughed. "I'm hardly in distress, Dr. Quinn."

"Just Ethan, and no, you're not in distress, but a cool drink would do us both good. Jumping off car batteries in the middle of July is thirsty work." He touched his hand to the small of her back as a subtle indication that he wasn't taking no for an answer. A gentle nudge, and Samantha relented.

After settling in at the diner's lunch counter, he ordered two sweet teas with lots of ice, each with a sprig of mint and a slice of lemon.

He glanced over at Samantha to see her eyes closed, enjoying the blissful feel of the AC as she fanned the collar on her white blouse. When he'd seen her bent over the hood of her car, her snug skirt lovingly hugging her luscious derrière, he'd almost swallowed his tongue. "Have dinner with me this weekend." *Well, that just popped out.* But now that it was out there, he'd go with it.

Her eyes flew open as she shot him a confused look. "What? Why?"

"Why? Why does a man ask a woman out? I like you." He shrugged.

"You like me? You don't know me." She shook her head, taking a generous gulp of the sweet tea the waitress set in front of her before pressing the cool glass to her forehead.

He took a swig from his own. Ruby new her way around southern sweet tea.

"Well, maybe I don't know you that well, but I like what I see." He studied her face a moment before continuing. "I like how you move when I see you at college gatherings. I like how when you talk to someone you make them seem as if they are the only person in the room. Even Dr. DeHaven," he added with a smile.

"He's a lonely old man who just wants to be valued, acknowledged," she said with a shoulder lift.

Dr. DeHaven was the former dean of their college. Somewhere between seventy-five and ninety-five years old, he wore a lamentable toupee and ill-fitting false teeth. And he smelled like licorice.

"I like how you wear that gorgeous red hair of yours in ponytail, and the way you dress—simple, straightforward, and sexy. And I like how your green eyes light up when you receive a compliment. Like they did just now."

Her cheeks filled with color as she glanced down at the bar. "Thanks, but I don't think so."

He wouldn't tell her about the betting pool at the college

on who she'd go out with first. He hadn't participated, though he knew his name had been tossed in by some of his colleagues—his secretary Melinda for one. "Because?"

"It's not a good idea. We're in the same college . . ."

"But not in the same department, and neither of us reports to the other. We wouldn't be breaking any rules."

"Maybe not university rules."

"What then, your rules?"

"I don't think dating colleagues is sensible. Ever hear the phrase, 'Don't dip your pen in the company ink?'" she asked, a single brow lifted in challenge.

Ethan snorted. "Around here we say, 'Don't get your honey where you get your money.'" He drained the last of his sweet tea.

"Same difference," she muttered. "Besides, I don't have time. I'm working on a research project that requires my full attention."

He turned his body to face hers. "Your research is on love, is it not?" he asked with a raised brow. "What better way to conduct primary research than by going on a date. Put your theories to the test."

This time she snorted. "I only have one theory: This thing you call love, and I call compatibility, is nothing more than a chemical reaction."

"I agree there must be chemistry." He waggled his finger between the two of them. "We have it. In spades."

She let out a sardonic laugh and shook her head.

"But there's much more to love than just chemistry."

"Like?" she asked, skepticism clear in her voice.

"Romance."

"Romance? All those novels and poetry you teach gone to your head?"

"Perhaps. But romance is more than words on a page." He thought about his parents' long, happy marriage. "Romance is the little things you do to show someone you love them. Holding hands in the movies, a piece of chocolate on her pillow at night, an impromptu dance in the kitchen."

She propped her chin in her hand and studied his face. "You really are a hopeless romantic, aren't you?"

"Well, I don't know about hopeless."

Her phone buzzed with an incoming text. Pulling it out of her bag, she read the screen. "Car's ready." She stood up and began digging in her purse again.

"I've got it." He tossed some bills on the counter.

"Thank you. I owe you."

"Then have dinner with me, and we'll call it even."

She held up her index finger. "One dinner. My treat. And no romance."

Tossing her keys onto the kitchen counter, she opened the fridge and reached in for a cold bottle of water. She felt a twinge of guilt for the environment as she turned down the thermostat in her townhouse. Kicking off her shoes, she checked her voice messages. Nothing interesting. Some telemarketers, a researcher at NYU she planned to meet up with at a conference later this year, and her mother.

Padding barefoot into the living room, she dropped onto the sofa. What a day. She'd lost a promising graduate assistant who'd decided to move back to Los Angeles to be closer to her boyfriend, she had issues with data for a study she'd hoped to be closing soon, and another study hadn't been selected to receive a grant she'd been counting on.

Then there was the whole car fiasco. And the too-sexy-for-his-own-good—and hers—Ethan Quinn.

Propping her feet on the coffee table, she looked around. She really needed to finish unpacking the boxes that were lining the dining area wall.

She'd taken the associate professor position at the small, private university because she needed a change of pace. Especially after Craig dumped her. *After* he'd cheated on her with one of his students.

Her parents had been appalled that she would leave a secure teaching position at NYU to move to what amounted to rural Georgia in their eyes. But Sterling University was well-funded, had a strong commitment to academic freedom, a manageable-sized student body, and was considered one of the Southern Ivy League schools, on par with universities like Duke and Vanderbilt. And, more importantly, they were interested in taking her discovery to market.

Nestled in the hills of Northeast Georgia, the town of Sterling owed its existence to two things: granite and knowledge. Granite because it held some of the richest granite quarries in the world. If it was made of granite, it probably came from Sterling.

Knowledge, because Sterling University educated almost fourteen thousand students inside its hallowed halls, and sent them out into the world to share that knowledge.

Founded in 1835 by wealthy granite quarry magnate and town-founder, Samuel Sterling, who endowed the university with one million dollars and three hundred and fifty acres of land adjacent to the family home, the university's arts department even offered classes in granite carving. When the last of the Sterling line, Victoria Eliza Sterling-Pickard, died in 1974, she left the family home to the University for its use as its main administration building, aptly named Sterling Hall.

If you lived in or around Sterling, you most likely either worked for the university, or for one of the many granite quarries or monument makers.

Frankly, after the fast-paced life of New York City, she found the college town to be rather charming. It allowed her to focus on her work and held few distractions—unless you counted Ethan Quinn.

Her phone chimed with an incoming FaceTime call. Her mother, no doubt.

She rose and walked to the kitchen where she'd left her phone. Swiping her finger across the screen, she took the phone with her back to the sofa. Her mother's face came into view.

"Hi, Mom."

"Samantha, don't you look like something the cat dragged in. Don't let small-town living turn you into a slob."

Sam heard her father's startled laugh in the background. "Mom, I've had a rough day. My car wouldn't start after work. And it's hot here."

"I don't know why you don't get yourself a new car."

"For the same reason I've told you a thousand times: I don't make enough money yet." She'd already strapped herself with a mortgage and bought new furniture, since Craig kept theirs when she moved out. She didn't need a car payment to top it off. Not that she would ask for their help, but her parents were of the belief that a child needed to make her own way in the world. So, her wildly successful parents would not be offering to put her in a shiny new Mercedes anytime soon.

"I don't know why you don't join me and your father in our field," her mother admonished for the umpteenth time, her face disappearing from the screen as she reached for something. Ah, her daily intake of Scotch.

Sam cringed. Working in sex therapy with your parents. Like that wouldn't be awkward.

"I don't know how your father and I managed to have such a sexually repressed daughter," she continued, the highball glass poised for a sip.

Her father's disembodied voice said, "I don't want to know about my daughter's sex life, repressed or otherwise."

Her mother sighed. "World-renowned sex therapist shy about sexuality? It's a perfectly normal human function, as you very well know."

"So is my daughter's digestion, but that doesn't mean I want to talk about it."

"I'm not sexually repressed," Sam muttered. Okay, maybe a little sexually *insecure*. Once men discovered whose daughter she was, they assumed she was loose. Or really good in bed. Neither could be further from the truth.

The only daughter of the Masters and Johnson research team of the twenty-first century, Drs. Vincent and Katherine Love, she grew up in a home where sex was candidly discussed. She spent her teenage and college years living with the stigma that, since her parents were sex therapists, she must be a nymphomaniac. Guys pursued her with this —and *only* this—in mind. As a result, she'd had little to do with the opposite sex. Until Craig, that is.

His engineer's brain worked a lot like hers. She had thought that he understood her. Until he'd broken up with her saying she was frigid.

She wasn't frigid. She just wasn't . . . passionate. *Sue me.*

She thought about Ethan's comment, *Romance is the little things you do to show someone you love them.*

Her parents' relationship was more like a business enterprise, especially since their divorce. There had never been any romance, none of the subtle gestures Ethan had referred to. She thought she'd had the same no-nonsense relationship with Craig. Comfortable. Steady.

Minimalistic.

Or . . . clinical, even.

No, the Drs. Love, name and careers notwithstanding, were not the best role models for Ethan's romantic philosophy.

"Of course, what does it matter? What could you possibly find in that town to stir even the slightest of desires?"

"Mom."

"Well, you've cloistered yourself away from people your own age, your own marital status . . . I don't know how you expect to meet someone with whom you have anything in common. Someone who'll be your life partner. Like your father and me."

"But you're divorced."

"Pfft. We're still partners."

"Yeah, who live in the same house and date other people."

"It works for us. Now back to you. You've sentenced yourself to this celibate existence, and all because Craig didn't know what he had in you," her mom continued. "That's all I'm saying on the subject."

Right. *For now.* "Look, Mom, I've got some papers to grade. I'll talk to you and Dad soon."

"Bye, Samantha." The screen went blank. Tossing her phone on the sofa beside her, she leaned back and closed her eyes. Her thoughts returned to Ethan, and his brown eyes, the way his hair fell across his forehead. His contagious laughter.

What had she been thinking when she'd agreed to go to dinner with him? He'd caught her at a vulnerable moment. He'd helped her out, and she felt like she owed him.

So she'd pay her debt, and that would be that. No romance needed.

That should be easy. She didn't know how to do romance anyway.

2

After following Samantha home, Ethan took the main road to the other side of town, and the origins of his blue-collar roots. His mom had asked him to dinner—fried chicken, homemade mashed potatoes, green beans fresh from the garden, and apple crisp. That was an invitation he couldn't pass up.

Since his father's sudden death six months earlier, he'd been worried about his mother. His parents had been married almost forty years, and she'd all but built her life around him.

His father, Thomas, had loved reading, but never had the money to pursue an education. It was his love of reading that infused his son with the desire to study literature. Thomas had been employed by the Sterling Granite Quarry since he was old enough to work and was eventually promoted to foreman. Ethan's mother, Margaret, had been a housewife, raising their two kids, Ethan and his older sister Charlotte, on their father's modest income.

Charlotte couldn't wait to get out of Sterling. She went

away to college in California and never looked back. She now lived in Vancouver with her husband. The last time he had seen her was for their father's funeral.

Ethan had stayed in Sterling out of guilt over leaving his parents alone after his sister left. He'd attended Sterling University, playing baseball on a full scholarship—the only way he could have afforded an education, and after earning his Ph.D., he'd stayed on to teach, later becoming chair of the Literature and Creative Writing Department for Sterling's College of Arts and Sciences.

Arriving in the section of town known as Graniteville, for its proximity to the many successful granite quarries in Sterling, Ethan stopped at the pedestrian crosswalk in front of Parker Monuments, and waited for two boys to ride their bikes across the street. Not much had changed in Graniteville since his boyhood. Parker Monuments was still the largest headstone and monument maker in the region, the granite quarries and factories still offered the almost-five-thousand permanent residents gainful employment, the high school football stadium still featured the granite seats installed in 1961, and his mom still lived in the same house he'd grown up in.

Pulling into the driveway of the modest red brick house, he switched off the ignition. Just like the town, his childhood home hadn't changed. His father's 1965 powder-blue Chevy pickup sat in the yard off the driveway, while his mother's 2000 Chevrolet Impala sat in the carport.

His mom couldn't bring herself to sell the truck yet, even though its pristine condition would fetch a nice price.

The narrow front porch still boasted the metal mint-green and white glider. Some folks would call it retro. He just called it old. It had been his grandparents' before they'd passed it along to his parents.

He'd spent many a summer night on that glider trying his hand at romance. In fact, his first kiss was on that glider, with Alyssa Gartner, the prettiest girl in his eighth-grade class.

The front door opened and his mother stepped out, wiping her hands on a towel.

Climbing out of the car, he returned her wave. "Hi, Mom."

"What are you doing sitting in the car?"

"Oh, just reminiscing." He climbed the steps then leaned down to kiss her cheek. Margaret Quinn still bore the beauty of her youth. Dark-brown hair with a smattering of gray, smooth creamy skin, and warm brown eyes that lit up when she laughed.

He knew it was far too soon, but he hoped she would find love again someday. She had so much to give, and she had a lot of living left to do.

Dinner already graced the family dining table. What had once seated four, and on many occasions a couple more of his friends, was now set for two.

"Smells great, Mom. And biscuits!"

She patted his cheek. "Your favorite—cheddar drop biscuits."

They talked about the happenings in Sterling, the upcoming fall semester at the university, and Charlotte and her husband Drew's upcoming vacation to Europe. Charlotte's art gallery had recently had a successful show, and Drew's car dealership had posted some good numbers lately, so they were splurging.

After gorging on his mom's handiwork, he settled back with a fresh glass of tea. There was a certain subject he wanted to broach with her.

"Mom, have you thought about getting a job? Just something to get you out of the house?"

"A job? But I don't have any skills."

"Of course you do. You took care of the household finances for years, you volunteered at the public library, and you helped with the books for the gift shop at the hospital. You were PTA treasurer for three years. You've got skills."

"But a job?" She shook her head. "I don't know. Where would I find a job?"

"It just so happens the Department of Social Sciences is looking for a part-time receptionist, three days a week."

"Ethan," she admonished, "I don't have a resume or anything."

"Don't need one. I already spoke with Penny Dawson, the chair's assistant, and she wants to meet you on Wednesday."

She stood from the table and picked up their plates. He knew that tactic. She was thinking about it. She just needed a little nudge.

"You're bright and personable, you're organized, and you like people. You'd be perfect for the job."

He could practically see the wheels turning as she rinsed dishes at the sink.

Carrying the platter of chicken and the half-empty bowl of potatoes over to the counter, he began filling saver dishes with the leftovers. "We could even have dinner on the nights you work."

His mom glanced over her shoulder, a smile playing around her mouth. "I'd like that."

"Me, too." He took a dishtowel out of the drawer and began drying. "At least say you'll talk to Penny, then see how it goes." He gave her a slight hip check, and she laughed.

She patted his cheek as only a mother can do. "I'll think about it."

"WANT to catch a movie over in Carlyle tonight?" Delaney Driscoll asked, as Sam waited for her to shut down her computer. They were about to head over to Ruby's for lunch.

Delaney, a creative writing professor, and Sam had hit it off immediately despite their disparate outlooks on life. They'd met at a campus meeting for the American Association of University Women a week after Sam had moved to town and went for drinks that same night. Delaney already felt like the sister Sam never had.

"Can't. I have plans," she said, trying to put on a poker face.

"What kind of plans?" Delaney pressed, as she stuffed papers into a tote bag that read IF A WORD IN THE DICTIONARY WERE MISSPELLED, HOW WOULD WE KNOW?

Dammit, now she'd have to fess up. "I have a date."

"A date? With who?" She cringed. "Not that guy in archaeology who talks about dead people all the time?"

She hesitated, biting her lip. If she didn't tell Delaney who her date was with, she'd never hear the end of it. "No, um, it's with Ethan Quinn."

Delaney dropped the bag on her desk and grabbed Sam's shoulders. "Shut. Up! Ethan Quinn? Dreamy literature professor, Ethan Quinn?"

"Why? Do you know another Ethan Quinn?"

"Do you know how many women—and even a few men —would kill for a date with Ethan Quinn?"

"I suppose," Sam replied, shrugging noncommittally.

"Okay, how did this happen? I need details," Delaney prodded, then returned to the task of stuffing her tote.

Sam didn't really feel like sharing details. She shrugged. "I had a dead battery. He helped me out."

"He jumped you off?"

Sam cringed. "Why do people use that phrase? It's so . . . sexual."

Delaney snickered. "Now, why would you think that?"

"He gave my battery a jumpstart."

"And that's when he asked you out?"

"Well, no. He followed me to Bart's—"

"Aww. How chivalrous."

Sam rolled her eyes.

"Then he asked you out?"

"No. Bart's was busy so we walked over to Ruby's for a drink."

"And that's when he asked you out?" Delaney pressed on.

"Do you want me to tell the story or not?"

"Fine," Delaney said, indicating that Sam should continue.

"So, we were sitting at the counter and he asked me out."

"And?"

"And that's it." Sam tucked a lock of hair behind her ear and tried to look nonchalant.

"Some storyteller you are. No 'he said this,' and 'you said that,' no 'he touched my hand and my heart skipped a beat.' No descriptions, nothing. You'd flunk my beginners' creative writing course." Delaney wore a disappointed expression on her face. "Did he kiss you?"

Sam released an uncomfortable laugh. "No. Why would he do that?"

"Because he couldn't resist your pouty lips."

"You read too many romance novels."

"And you, my friend, don't read enough of them," Delaney suggested.

"I don't read *any*."

"My point exactly." Shouldering the bag, Delaney glanced around the office then headed for the door, Sam on her heels, hoping the conversation was over.

"What are you wearing?" Delaney asked as she flipped off the lights. "Wait, where are you going?"

"Some restaurant and marina north of here." Sam pulled the door closed behind her and came alongside Delaney as they walked down the corridor.

"Dave's. Okay, so it's not exactly swanky, but it could be fun. You should wear something that says fun and breezy, but not too sleazy."

"What?" Sam choked out a laugh.

"You know, a sundress with some cute strappy sandals maybe."

Sam shook her head. "I don't have a sundress and cute strappy sandals. What's wrong with what I'm wearing now?" Sam glanced down at her navy pencil skirt, pale ivory blouse, and Sam Edelman ballets.

Delaney stopped, took a step back, a dubious expression on her face. "That? No, that won't do. You look too . . . buttoned up. This isn't New York." She checked her watch. "We have time."

"For what?"

"A little post-lunch shopping excursion."

❧

ETHAN PULLED his car up in front of Samantha's townhouse and slid it into park. Grabbing the bouquet of multicolored zinnias off the passenger seat, he got out and walked to her door.

The red-brick townhouse was in Georgetown Square, one of the newer neighborhoods that had sprung up around the university campus and had quickly become a favorite of faculty and administrative staff for its proximity. The townhomes' Georgian-style architecture, with its classical proportions, black shutters, and white trim, fit the town of Sterling. A rich glossy red front door on Samantha's place added impact.

Ringing the bell, he looked around at the neighborhood, appreciating the quiet, tree-lined streets, thinking it would be a great place to raise a family.

The door opened, and he turned to see a vision that rendered him momentarily speechless. Samantha stood in the doorway wearing a soft floral sundress in shades similar to those of the zinnias he held—rich reds, smoky pinks, and deep violets. Her flaming-red hair floated around her in soft waves. Sexy, feminine, and flirty.

He couldn't help himself, a whistle escaped before he could give her a proper greeting. "Hi."

"Hi," she said, the corners of that full mouth tugging upward.

"You look . . . incredible."

"Thanks." She glanced at the flowers. "Are those for me?"

"Oh, yes." He held out the bouquet. *Smooth, real smooth, Quinn. Come on, man, it's not like it's your first rodeo.*

Confusion furrowed her brow. "No one's ever given me flowers," she muttered.

"Well then, shame on them." *How is it that this beautiful*

woman had never received flowers from a man? "Are you ready?"

"Yes. Let me, uh, go put these in some water. Come in." She left him to make his way inside.

To the left was a tidy living area furnished with modern pieces upholstered in what looked like a soft taupe leather. To the right was a study, the black lacquer desk scattered with papers. Straight ahead through the foyer, on the other side of the stairs, he spied the kitchen.

Samantha stood at the sink filling a colorful hand-blown glass vase with water. A stack of boxes on the other side of the kitchen caught his eye.

"Yeah, I haven't finished unpacking yet." She laughed, sounding a bit nervous. "I guess whatever's in those boxes isn't a necessity, because I haven't missed anything." She dropped the flowers into the vase, loosely arranging them. "There. I guess that's all they need, right?"

"They'll be fine."

Carrying the flowers out to the living room, she breezed past him, leaving a subtle fragrance of jasmine behind. As she placed the vase in the center of a black lacquer coffee table, he took the opportunity to explore the space. Along the wall opposite the sofa stood a bookcase filled with books, mostly psychology tomes with a few mysteries thrown in for good measure. French doors opened onto a screened back porch, with a modest back-yard beyond that.

"Can I get you something to drink?" Sam asked, as she turned toward him.

"I thought we'd head out to dinner."

"Sure." Picking up a handbag and sweater, she led the way to the front door, giving him a view of her bare back. Smooth silky skin he knew would be warm to the touch beckoned him. *Slow down there, Quinn.* Yes, it had been a while, but he wasn't the caveman type.

Following her out, he walked around to the passenger side of his car to open the door for her. When she sat in the seat, the hem of her dress slid up to reveal a smooth thigh. Swallowing hard, Ethan tore his eyes away from that irresistible skin and closed the door.

Holy hell. He only hoped he could keep his hands off her long enough to have dinner.

THEY ARRIVED AT DAVE'S, a sprawling ranch-style building with a metal roof and a wraparound porch. Behind it, a large tree-lined lake dotted with boats served as scenery in the late-afternoon sun. To the right, a sidewalk led to a marina where more boats, everything from smallish fishing boats to larger pontoon boats, bobbed at their moorings.

Before Sam could get out of the car, Ethan had walked around to open her door. She glanced up at his handsome face—an errant lock of hair fell over his forehead, resulting in a devil-may-care look with his dark-wash jeans and green button-down shirt. Taking her hand, he helped her from the car. Tingles danced along her arm in response to his touch. Oh yes, they definitely had chemistry!

She knew from her research that hormones and neurotransmitters worked together to help humans find love. But she also knew that chemistry only arises when two people were being themselves. Unlike smiles, chemistry wasn't something you could fake.

Each stage of love, from attraction to romance to attachment, had its own set of hormones that were activated. And right now, the attraction hormones were giving her a buzz much like a cocaine high. A buzz that had been conspicuously absent with Craig.

Withdrawing her hand left her feeling bereft. Lonely. Not good, Sam thought. Not good at all. She didn't need this kind of complication in her life right now. She had a patent to pursue. A license agreement to negotiate. She didn't need a man to pursue. Or a relationship to negotiate.

And relationships inevitably led to sex, and sex often led to disappointment.

She headed in the direction of the restaurant.

"We're not going there," Ethan said. He held out his hand, indicating that they were going to the marina.

"But I thought we were having dinner." So I could pay my debt and move on, she thought.

"We are, but not here."

Placing his hand on the small of her back, he directed her along the sidewalk to the marina. Picking her way carefully along the boards of the dock, she silently cursed Delaney and her strappy-sandals idea. Any moment now, she expected one of her heels to take a dive into one of the cracks between the boards, and she'd take a header into the lake's dark waters.

"Here we are," Ethan said.

They'd stopped in front of one of the many pontoon boats docked at the marina.

"Is this yours?" she asked.

"Belongs to a buddy of mine." Taking her elbow, he helped her aboard. "Have a seat," he said, indicating the padded seats along the front railing of the boat. "And while those heels are sexy as hell, they aren't practical on a boat." He knelt at her feet, and taking her ankle in his hand, slipped off first one shoe and then the other. The electricity that shot up her legs could have lit the city of Atlanta for a week.

His warm brown gaze shot to her face. He'd felt it, too.

"Um, thank you." She broke the stare and bent down to slide her shoes out of the way. There had been something unsettlingly sexy about watching Ethan remove her shoes. As if *she* were the *voyeur*.

Ethan stood and moved around the boat, clearly at home, untying ropes and checking gauges before starting the engine. Steering the boat out of its covered slip, he headed out.

The craft looked to be about twenty-four, twenty-five feet long, with two wraparound seating areas in the bow and a captain's chair at the controls. Beneath a green-and-white-striped awning over the stern stood a table set with a red-and-white-checkered plastic tablecloth clipped to the table's edges, presumably to keep it from blowing off. Beyond the table sat a large cooler.

The sun slid behind the trees, taking most of the day's heat with it, making her glad she'd brought a lightweight cardigan.

As they picked up speed, she glanced back at Ethan, standing legs-apart against the bouncing of the boat, looking like he belonged on the water. Aviator sunglasses framed his eyes, and the wind blew his dark-brown locks in disarray, plastering his shirt to the broad chest and flat stomach underneath. A shiver ran up her spine, and it had nothing to do with the now-chilly breeze.

Turning her face into the wind, she gazed out at the lake's vast expanse. There were people on Sea-Doos, others waterskiing, and still others fishing along its shore.

She assumed from the partially set table and the cooler

that they would be dining on the boat. Just the two of them. All alone. Her stomach did a slow roll, nerves setting in.

It had been a while since she'd been on an actual "date." She and Craig had lived together for almost two years, and she couldn't recall any time during those two years ever going on what most people would consider a date.

As the boat slowed, Sam's nerves did the opposite, kicking up her heartbeat and pulse, making her wonder why she'd ever agreed to go out with Ethan Quinn.

3

─────

Ethan steered the boat around a bend to a cove surrounded on three sides by white pines, mountain laurel, and sugar maple. Cutting the engines, he moved to the back of the boat and dropped anchor. The boat bobbed on its own wake before the waves dissipated along the shore then settled into a gentle rocking motion.

"Now that we're anchored, I can play the proper host." Opening the cooler, he took a bottle of Veuve Clicquot from its nest in the ice. Then lifting the backseat, he plundered in the under-seat storage compartment for two disposable champagne flutes.

"I hope you like champagne," he said, as he popped the cork. Setting the flutes on the table, he poured the bubbly. Holding one out to her, he indicated that Samantha should join him in the stern. As she rose, the breeze flirted with the hem of her dress, flashing him with a silky thigh.

When he'd slipped off those sinful heels, he hadn't missed the warmth of her legs beneath his hand, the velvety skin, or the rich red nail polish on her toes. He loved a woman who pampered her feet, especially when she slid those pampered feet along his bare legs. Even her legs had smelled like jasmine.

She walked toward him with some hesitation.

"I won't bite, you know," he said, then took a sip from his drink. "Unless you want me to."

Her forward progress stopped, and he laughed. "Come on. I promise, no teeth."

Passing her the champagne, he gazed at her over the rim. "To soft summer nights," he toasted. She tapped her flute to his and turned it up.

"Mmm. Delicious." She licked her lips, and his brain momentarily malfunctioned. Where was he? *Who* was he? *Damn.* She'd been at the university since last fall, and now he was asking himself why he'd waited so long to ask her out.

"Are you hungry?" God knew he was, but not for food. "We have a chilled supper of crab salad followed by a peach gazpacho and cold poached salmon for the entree. And for dessert, bittersweet chocolate mousse."

She laughed, a bright, sparkling sound. "You have all that in the cooler?"

"Yep. But I can't take credit for any of it. Dave prepared the food."

"Dave? As in Dave's Restaurant?" She pointed in the direction of the marina, hidden behind the trees, then shook her head. "I thought it was more of a fish shack than fine dining."

"Oh, it is. But Dave is CIA-trained."

"Then . . . Why?"

He shrugged. "It's the family business. His father, David Lawrence, Sr., started the restaurant back in the sixties. It's been very successful, and you don't mess with success."

He watched as several expressions flitted across her face. Bemusement, amusement, and then understanding.

He refilled her glass and then set about the business of serving dinner. Retrieving white disposable dinnerware from the storage compartment, he set salad and dinner plates on the table, followed by flatware and napkins.

"Ma'am," he held the back of a chair. As she moved past him, her hair brushed his shoulder, and he wondered how those glossy strands would feel sliding across his bare chest.

Taking a seat, she placed the napkin in her lap. He gazed down at the bare skin and couldn't resist. Grazing his fingertips across her shoulder, it was all he'd expected and more. Smooth and warm. Her sharp intake of breath at his touch sent heat straight to his groin.

Step away from the sexy woman, his brain said. *Grab her and kiss her senseless*, his body said. His brain won out. *Damn brain.*

Glad to have something to occupy his hands, he plated the salads and opened a bottle of chardonnay, then took the chair opposite the lovely professor and poured the wine into cups.

The sun had set, ushering in dusk, so he lit a citronella candle he'd found in the storage compartment for both light and mosquito control.

"*Bon appetit*," he said, picking up his fork. He watched with pleasure as she tasted the delicate crab salad, a look of delight on her face. *Talk, man, talk. Get your mind out of the gutter.* "What brought you from NYU to the hills of Northeast Georgia?"

"Sterling University is expanding its Department of Social Sciences, so they contacted me about joining the faculty." She paused to sip her wine and looked as if she were going to say something else then changed her mind. "It was an offer I couldn't refuse. How did you end up here?"

"I grew up in Sterling, went to school here." He shrugged. "Then took a position here."

"You spent your entire college career here? All three degrees? That's unusual."

"I suppose. But I like it here. My parents were here. Sterling is an excellent university, and the town has a lot to offer. So why would I leave?"

"Were?"

Surprised she'd caught that, he hesitated. "Well, my mom is still here, but my dad passed away six months ago." The kick in the gut those words still delivered left him breathless.

Her eyes softened as she gazed at him with sympathy. "I'm so sorry. I'm sure that's been difficult."

"It has, especially since it was so sudden." At her questioning look, he explained, "Heart attack. What about your parents?"

She made a face then laughed, a nervous one this time. "My parents are still alive and living in upstate New York."

Her response was vague, but he let it go. He knew who her parents were. Everyone at the university knew. It was one of the juvenile reasons for the betting pool. "And, as we determined the other day, Dr. Love, your research is on . . . love. A fitting topic for you given your name."

"Yes, well. I wouldn't say my topic is love, but rather compatibility. What brings two people together and what makes them stay together."

He shrugged. "Love."

She shook her head. "Sometimes love isn't enough. Just because you 'love' someone," she put air quotes around the word, "doesn't mean you'll be compatible. Compatibility is all about biology. Chemistry."

"Yes, so you said the other day."

"And you said there was more to love than chemistry."

"Yes, I did." He thought about his parents. "Romance."

She shook her head again and laughed that cynical laugh he'd heard in Ruby's Diner the other day. "And why the air quotes?"

"Around the word 'love' you mean?" At his nod, she continued, "I don't believe in love."

Reaching across the table, he took her hand, his thumb brushing along her skin. "What, or should I say who, Dr. Love, has made you so cynical when it comes to matters of the heart?"

"Matters of the heart?" She snorted, as she withdrew her hand. She didn't consider herself cynical. Just practical. "That's a romantic notion perpetuated by jewelry stores, florists, and chocolatiers. True biological compatibility has nothing to do with the heart and everything to do with evolution and survival of the species."

He scoffed. "Anyone can reproduce. Two complete strangers can ensure the perpetuation of the species. But it takes a strong relationship to see the couple, and their family, through good times and bad."

"Well, at least we agree on something. But love has little to do with whether a couple has a strong bond."

"Right." He rose from the table and took away the salad plates. Taking two small containers out, he removed the lids, and as he set them on top of the dinner plates, he continued, "You contend it's just chemistry."

She looked up into his brown eyes that held a challenge to her theory. "Yes," she said, brow lifted, accepting that challenge.

Before he took his seat, he walked up to the bow of the boat and retrieved her sweater. "You look chilly." He draped it around her shoulders then rested his hands there.

The thoughtfulness of the gesture touched her, and the warmth of his hands penetrated the light knit material. "Thank you." He squeezed her shoulders then walked around the table to his chair, his expression smug. *Oh, no you don't, Dr. Quinn.* "I see what you did there." She picked up her spoon and wagged it at him then dipped into her gazpacho. Sweet peaches, mild cucumber, and bright cilantro teased her tongue.

"What did I do?" he asked, looking innocent.

"You're trying to prove your point by doing something thoughtful."

"No, I'm trying to keep you from catching pneumonia."

Sam snorted. "Right. Pneumonia in July. And you know as well as I do that you don't catch pneumonia from being chilly."

"Even so, you said thank you."

"I was just being polite."

"Uh-huh. Like when I gave you the flowers. Admit it, you were touched."

She shrugged. "It was nice. No one has ever given me flowers."

"Which reminds me, how is that even possible? What kind of men have you been dating?"

This was a road she didn't intend to go down. "Practical, educated men."

"But not very smart, if you ask me."

"Craig was an MIT-educated engineer." As soon as the words were out of her mouth, she wished she could take them back. She hadn't planned on discussing Craig.

"Craig? Since you referred to him in the past-tense, and you're here with me, I'm assuming the relationship is over."

She set her spoon in the now-empty container and placed her hands in her lap. Upbringing notwithstanding, the soup had been so good she yearned to turn up the bowl and drink the little bit that remained. "Yes."

"And how long did Craig last?"

"Almost two years."

"Two years, and the man never brought you flowers?"

"No."

"As I said, dumbass."

"Our relationship wasn't like that. We were . . . partners . . . helpmates—"

Ethan snorted. "Doesn't sound like a relationship at all. Sounds more like roommates."

Sam bristled, then calmed. The truth hurt. "And you, Casanova, how long was your last relationship?"

He rose from the table, removing the containers. "About the same as yours."

"And did you bring her flowers?"

"Of course."

"Didn't seem to have solidified your relationship." She turned in her chair to watch him. She liked the way he moved. He had an economy of motion—efficient, but graceful.

"No, I suppose it didn't. But bringing her flowers made me happy, and she seemed to enjoy them."

Taking a platter out of the cooler, he removed the cellophane to reveal two beautiful salmon steaks with a creamy dill sauce, dressed with slender asparagus spears. He plated the entrees in silence, and she let his comment go, focusing instead on the delectable salmon, the crisp chardonnay, and the sounds of nature.

The night sky had gone purple, creating silhouettes of the trees and setting the stage for a chorus of frogs and crickets. The candle in the center of the table flickered, casting shadows and light across Ethan's face.

He'd clearly worked hard creating a scene most women would melt over. She didn't want to appear ungrateful. "Dinner is delicious. Dave is wasting his talents."

"Perhaps, but family is important to him. He does have plans to open a second restaurant in Sterling. Something casual, but offering upscale food." He stabbed an asparagus spear, bringing it to his mouth.

"Sounds like you know him pretty well."

"We went to high school together."

Sam didn't know what it was like to have long-term relationships. Not just with guys, but with girls, too. Her parents moved around a lot. Chasing careers in academia sometimes meant moving from institution to institution. They rarely stayed for more than two or three years before some other prestigious institution came calling offering bigger lab space, more support staff, and more money. They'd been at Cornell the longest—five years now.

"So, you must have research that backs up your theory," Ethan said, interrupting her thoughts.

"I do. It's the reason I'm here. Sterling University is very interested in this research."

"Why is that?"

"Because it's groundbreaking, and because I brought patent-ready IP for a blood test."

Ethan sat back, set his fork on his plate, and wiped his mouth with his napkin. "A blood test? What kind blood test?"

"I call it a compatibility assay. It can determine who your match is."

"You mean like an organ donor?"

"Yes, but for relationship compatibility."

"All right, I'll bite. How do you determine someone's compatibility with a blood test?"

"I can't give you details, since my patent application is still pending, but I *can* say that there are certain chemicals in the blood that indicate who will be a good biological match."

Humans are often attracted to people who possess a particular set of genes called major histocompatibility complex, or MHC. MHC plays a critical role in the ability to fight viruses. Mates with dissimilar MHC genes produce healthier offspring with broad immune systems.

Sam had discovered a blood chemical, which she called MHC-P1 that predicts MHC, and through her current research, she'd proven that couples whose MHC-P1 were on opposite ends of the spectrum, indicating their MHC genes were dissimilar, not only had healthier, more productive children, but they also had longer, happier relationships.

"And you've proven this how?"

"My research studies. By taking blood samples, conducting interviews with, and administering compatibility questionnaires to, happily attached couples who have been together twenty years or more."

"Compatibility questionnaires? You mean like the ones online dating services use?"

"Correct. I have a control group of some five thousand

couples married for at least twenty years. I've given them the questionnaire and taken blood. A statistically significant percentage of those who report that they are happily married—or otherwise attached—show strong chemical compatibility, similar to that of the questionnaires."

"I also have a cohort," of which she was one, but she didn't tell him that, "of some forty-eight hundred single or divorced men and women who have taken the same questionnaire and blood test. When I take blood, I run the tests against those individuals in the database, and when I find matches, I compare the chemical compatibility to the questionnaire compatibility."

"A statistically significant percentage of the time, the blood chemistry inversely matches, and the compatibility questionnaires match as well."

Once she completes her research, and the university obtains the patent, SoulMates.com, a popular online dating service, was very interested in licensing her "compatibility assay," which they would like to offer their users for an additional fee.

"Impressive." He sat back and crossed his arms over his chest. "You've taken love, with all its mystery and beauty, and reduced it to something as romantic as a cholesterol test."

"I'd prefer to think I've removed all the barriers, pitfalls, and heartaches people encounter on the road to finding a lasting relationship."

"Sign me up then." He sat up and slapped the table with his hand.

"Excuse me?"

"Are you still enrolling people in your single-slash-divorced cohort?"

"Yes."

"Then sign me up. Take my blood. Give me the compatibility questionnaire."

Holy crap. He was serious.

SHE HAD A DEER-IN-HEADLIGHTS LOOK. "OKAY." Then she blinked. "Are you sure?"

"I can come by your lab on Monday around three-thirty, after my last class."

"I'd have to check my schedule." She bit her lip. "I think that should work."

"Good. Now that that's settled, how about some dessert?"

She nodded, still appearing stunned by his request to join her study. She'd become animated when she talked about her research. The glow of pride looked good on her.

Ethan rose from the table and, opening the cooler, reached in for the two parfait glasses filled with creamy chocolate mousse and topped with shaved dark chocolate.

Handing her a glass and a spoon, he reassumed his place across from her. "More wine?"

"No, thank you." He watched as she took a bite of the sweet mousse with the bitter dark chocolate shavings then closed her eyes in ecstasy. "Mmm. Oh my! Talk about patents! Dave should patent this dessert." She opened her eyes and pointed her spoon at the glass.

He'd felt that hum of pleasure all the way to his groin, but he knew what she meant. The sweet and bitter collided on your tongue, creating an explosion of tastes.

"Yeah, this is his specialty. It's the one thing he added to the restaurant's menu, and it's been a big hit." He took another bite, his gaze focused on her mouth, where a morsel of dark chocolate rested. Before he gave it any thought, he stood and, leaning over the table, licked the chocolate from her mouth. The spark he felt when his tongue met her lips might have come from sticking his tongue in a light socket.

He retreated, gazed into her surprised green eyes then advanced once more. This time he pressed his lips to hers, a soft caress, before diving in. His tongue parted her lips to tangle with hers, tasting the chocolate. No other part of their bodies touched, just lips and tongues, and the headiness of it raced through his blood, pooled low in his belly, and made him dizzy with want. *Sweet Jesus.*

This wasn't just chemistry. This was a conflagration.

Her spoon clattered to the boat deck, and her hand found its way into his hair, as she moaned low in her throat. Reaching down, he groped his way around until he found the glass of mousse she still held in her hand and set it on the table before it followed the fate of the spoon. Lifting her hand, he pulled her from her chair and up against him, no longer content with just their lips touching.

Grasping her hips, he held her against him, where she could feel every inch of what she did to him. Her other hand wrapped around his neck, playing with the hair at his nape, sending shivers along his spine, as she groaned and tried to get closer still. His leg slipped between hers as he drew her up his body.

Sliding his hands up her ribs, he broke the kiss and pressed his lips to the pulse in her neck, fluttering like a hummingbird's wings. The gentle rocking of the boat intensified his arousal.

He had to stop this before he dragged her down to the deck, ripped off that sundress, and buried himself deep inside her.

One last nip at her neck, then a flick of his tongue over

her lips, and he stepped back. Her eyes flew open, and the look of desire he saw in them almost swept his resolve.

A flash of lightning and a rumble of thunder in the distance spurred him to action. "We'd better head back."

Her hand rose to her lips, lingered there. "Right." She wore that dazed look again, but for a different reason this time. His male pride gloated a little.

At least the ride back to the marina would give him a chance to lose the screaming erection he had. He just had to think of something unappealing. Like the time he'd walked in on his grandmother in her underwear. Yep. That should do it.

"THANK YOU FOR DINNER. I had a nice time," Sam said, hand on the car door latch, ready to bolt.

"Don't run away, little girl." In the dark car interior, Sam could hear the laughter in his voice. "What kind of gentleman would I be if I didn't walk a beautiful woman to her door. Especially when that beautiful woman neglected to turn on her porch light."

"Bulb's burned out," Sam responded. "I can't reach it without a stepladder. Which I don't have."

"Then it's a good thing I'm here to ensure the bogeyman doesn't get you."

He opened the door and made his way around the front of the car to open Sam's door.

"I'm quite capable of opening my own door," she said as she took his hand. "And getting out of the car by myself."

"No one said you weren't. Just gives me an excuse to hold your hand." He winked, making her glad he held her hand to steady her as her knees threatened to give way. His hand now at the small of her back, he followed her up the walk.

When she reached her door, she fumbled with the keys, hoping to unlock the door and get inside the house before he had an opportunity to kiss her again. Something about his kisses switched off all higher-functioning parts of her brain, leaving only her reptilian instinct in control—a little like leaving a teenager at home without adult supervision. For an entire weekend. With a cabinet full of liquor.

Just as she thought she was free, Ethan stepped up behind her, his hands settling at her waist, his lips pressed to her bare shoulder. An involuntary shiver coursed down her spine.

"Samantha, I'd really like to see you again."

"Hmmm." She lowered her chin, giving him easier access. He nibbled his way around to her ear, and she leaned against him for support. Her legs had suddenly turned to a quivering mass of Jell-O. And the unsupervised teenager just invited all her friends to a house party.

He turned her to face him and captured her mouth with his, and she knew she'd lost the battle. His tongue touched hers, and her fingers found their way into the front of his shirt, grasping onto it like a life preserver in a stormy sea. The scent of fresh air, soap, and full-blooded male assaulted her senses.

Her blood hummed through her body like electricity through a powerline. Never. It had never been like this. She wanted to wrap herself around him, feel the heat of him, the taste of him. He pressed her back against the door, trapping her between his delicious heat and her erstwhile escape route.

When he released her, disappointment swamped her. A

chill crossed her body in the absence of his warmth, leaving her bereft.

"Good night, Sam," he murmured against her ear. "I'll see you Monday."

Too dazed to speak, she let herself into her house and closed the door behind her, slumping against it. Ethan Quinn should be on the FBI's Most Wanted list. With kisses like that, he was armed and dangerous.

4

Whistling a happy tune, Ethan parked in front of Granite Fitness. His evening with the smart, beautiful, and slightly uptight Samantha Love had gone swimmingly. He couldn't have written a better script for romance.

And the kiss good night? Well, let's just say he'd spent a good ten minutes in a cold shower after he'd gotten home.

After retrieving his gym bag from the trunk, he headed into the center where he was meeting Nash Taylor, his best friend from high school and Sterling Bobcats head football coach. Sterling University's fledgling NCAA Division I program had proved to be an upstart in only its second year. With Nash's third season coming up, fans had high hopes for the Football Championship Subdivision.

After checking in, Ethan spotted Nash running on the treadmill, wiping his face with a towel. Nash still had the physique of an NFL player, but a season-ending injury his fifth season as a highly drafted starting quarterback for the Denver Broncos forced him to treat his body with a kinder, gentler workout, a far cry from the training he'd done as a pro. Not that most people would notice the difference.

"'Bout time you got here, Quinn."

"You almost finished?"

"Just getting warmed up. I thought I'd kick your ass in a little bench-press competition this morning. Think your college-professor form can handle it?"

"Bring it on." Ethan climbed onto the StairMaster next to Nash, punched in his preferences, and started climbing like it was the final approach to the summit. Feeling Nash's eyes on him, he looked over. "What?"

"Someone ate their Wheaties this morning."

"Just feeling good."

"Hiya, Nash," one of the local gym bunnies called out. Nash waved, but Ethan knew Nash preferred women with a lot more upstairs. And he wasn't talking about boobs.

Single, and some not-so-single women, went crazy over Nash's blond hair, all-American face, and disarming smile. He could've had his pick of any one of them, but he chose to keep his distance.

"We'll see how good you feel after I'm done with you." Nash slowed the treadmill to a crawl before stepping off. "I'll see you in the weight room."

Ethan welcomed the time alone with his thoughts. And his first was about Sam. He really liked her. He'd been giving more thought to settling down lately. Maybe having a couple of kids. He knew his mom wanted grandkids, and since his sister didn't appear to be in any hurry, it looked like it might be up to him to pass on the Quinn genes. Besides, he'd sowed enough wild oats already.

He wanted what his parents had had. Someone to come home to, someone who understood his world and wanted to share it. And Samantha Love more than fit the bill.

MONDAY AFTERNOON, Sam set out everything she needed to enroll Ethan in her study and to take a finger-stick blood sample. She straightened the consent form and pen, lined up the lancet, alcohol wipe, and capillary tube, then huffed out a breath of exasperation. Her nerves jangled like she was going on a first date.

And speaking of first dates, her date with Ethan had sent her into a tailspin. She couldn't get that good night kiss off her mind. Every time she tried to concentrate on the data she was analyzing, she'd see his warm brown eyes that crinkled at the corners when he laughed or recall the taste of his lips on hers.

Generally, kissing for her held the same level of interest as vanilla ice cream—she could take it or leave it. But kissing Ethan was like indulging in cookies 'n cream ice cream with extra chocolate sauce on top. And white chocolate sprinkles. Decadent. Sinful.

No kiss had ever rocked her world like that.

After her run yesterday, she'd come home to find a folded stepladder leaning against the wall and a pack of bulbs at her front door with one missing. His thoughtfulness touched something that she'd kept buried deep. No one ever took care of her. She always took care of herself, even if that meant calling a repairman. And that had been the second time he'd come to her aid.

She glanced at her watch. Three-fifteen. She really needed to find something to occupy her mind besides Ethan's kisses for the next fifteen minutes. She was a busy woman—surely she could find *something* to do.

A knock sounded on the doorframe of the open lab door, and she nearly jumped out of her skin.

"Hey there. You looked like you were in deep concentration." Delaney stood in the doorway. "What's up?" she asked, as she stepped into the room.

"Nothing. Nothing's up, why?"

Delaney chuckled. "Nervous much?"

Sam clasped her hands in front of her. "I'm not nervous."

"Okaaaay. This is the first chance I've had to see how your date with Dreamy Dr. Quinn went." Delaney's eyes sparkled with mischief.

"Fine. It went fine."

"Fine? Just fine?"

"It was nice." Sam waved her hand as if dismissing Ethan's soul-altering kiss.

"Nice? Sheesh." Delaney pulled up a lab stool and perched on it, and Sam groaned inwardly. "That sounds disappointing."

"I, uh, I have a research subject coming in," she glanced at her watch again, "five minutes."

"Okay. Chill. I'll leave when the subject gets here." Sam could feel Delaney's eyes on her face, and the longer she stared the hotter Sam's face felt. "Did he at least kiss you good night?"

A full-on flush swept over Sam as she thought back to that moment.

"Oh, yeah," Delaney said, wagging her finger at Sam. "I can tell by that blush that he did. And even more, you liked it. A lot."

"Knock, knock. I'm a little early. Am I interrupting? Is this a good time?"

Oh, for the love of chemistry—did he hear their conversation?

Delaney gasped, but Sam willed herself not to glance her way.

Ethan stood filling her doorway, his light-blue dress shirt open at the neck tucked into dark gray slacks, and hair looking tousled and sexy. A grin split his face. Clearly he'd heard.

"No. I mean, yes, this is a good time. Come in," Sam said with as much dignity as she could muster. Ethan moved into the room, glanced at Delaney and nodded, "Dr. Driscoll."

"Dr. Quinn," Delaney said on a sigh, then apparently came to her senses. "I'll just be going. Got some papers to grade." She hopped off the stool and gave Sam a look that said they'd talk later.

Ethan came around the lab desk to stand next to Sam, filling her vision. "I had a really nice time Friday night."

God, he smelled like heaven. "Yeah, me too. But I still owe you for helping with my car. And now the light bulb." *Now why did she have to say that?* She could have just let it go and been done with the all-too-attractive Dr. Quinn.

"Why is that?" He leaned a hip on the counter, bringing him within a couple of inches of touching her. Her pulse stuttered.

"I thought the plan for Friday was for me to buy you dinner." She stepped back. "That didn't happen."

"Well, if you insist on repaying me, go out with me tonight." He inched toward her again. "I'll even let you buy this time."

"I can't." She couldn't take another onslaught like Friday night. "I'm having dinner with Delaney." She pointed to the door where said scapegoat had exited only moments before. And now she'd *have* to have dinner with the scapegoat, *er*, Delaney, so she wouldn't be a liar.

Which meant Delaney would give her the third degree about Friday . . . and today. The lesser of two evils—or in this case, rock meet hard place.

"Tomorrow then." He inched closer. Every move she made away from him, he made up the distance. And she didn't have a lot of room in her ten-by-ten lab.

"Our department has a cocktail party to welcome the new anthropology professor." Retreat.

Advance. "Then you name the day."

Retreat. "I'm busy—all week."

Advance. "You're the one who feels the need to pay me back."

Retreat. *Damn.* She'd bumped into the lab stool that Delaney had just vacated and had nowhere else to go. "Fine. How about lunch?" Lunch would be safe. No good-night kisses. Or kisses across the table in broad daylight. "Wednesday?"

"I can do that." Advance.

With no other choice, she stood her ground. "Good. It's a date. I mean, I'll put it on my calendar."

Before he could say anything else, she said, "So, before I take your blood, I'll need to get your written consent to participate in the study." She picked up the paper form and handed it to him. "I explained the study to you Friday night." On the boat. Where you kissed me senseless. "But let's go over it again."

"Whatever you say, Dr. Love." He leaned over her shoulder to read the document, his scent nearly driving her mad. She had the sudden urge to bury her face in his neck and inhale.

She pointed out the salient points of the study as he drew closer and closer. She glanced up at him with annoyance then realized her mouth was only inches from his. *Crap! Look away from the delicious lips.* She cleared her throat and returned her attention to the form.

As the researcher for the study, she owed him, the

research subject, a clear and concise explanation of the study, but in a moment of self-preservation, she stepped back and said, "Please read the consent form and feel free to ask me any questions you might have before signing it."

She moved around him and busied herself with some nonsense just to get some distance.

"Done."

She turned around, saw his signature on the form, then lifted her eyes to his. "But you didn't even read it. Don't you have questions?"

"I trust you, Dr. Love." His face was earnest, but his eyes sparkled. Those eyes lowered to her mouth, and her legs wobbled.

"But you really should read documents before you sign them," she admonished, her brow furrowed in confusion.

"I'll take my chances here. Now you have to stick my finger, right?"

"Yes." She gathered the lancet, an alcohol wipe, and a small glass collection tube.

"Will it hurt?" he asked, feigning fear.

"You'll feel a quick stick, but it hurts no more than a pin prick."

He chuckled. "I think I can handle it, Dr. Love." She looked so professional . . . and hot in her white lab coat, light-gray blouse, and dark-gray pencil skirt. The killer heels she wore put her mouth just below his. He only had to lean forward an inch or two to claim it.

"Have a seat," she said, interrupting his thoughts. She pulled on a pair of gloves, while he perched on the lab stool.

"You'd be surprised how many people get light-headed from a little finger stick. Give me your middle finger."

He presented her with his right middle finger and flashed her a flirtatious grin.

She blinked but tore open the alcohol wipe, then bent over his hand and swiped the fingertip. Picking up the lancet, she gave his finger a quick jab then set about filling the glass tube. Her hands were warm through the latex gloves as she worked efficiently to complete her task.

Her hair slipped over her shoulders, brushing the back of his other hand where it rested on the countertop, and that flowery perfume filled his nose. He reached up, tucked her hair behind her ear, and her gaze lifted to his.

Green eyes with long dark lashes stared into his. Her lips parted, then her brow creased, and she returned her attention to his finger.

Finished with her collection, she opened a Band-Aid and wrapped it around his finger.

"So what happens next?" he asked.

"If you'd read the consent form, you'd know." She moved to a counter behind them that was lined with equipment.

"True enough. But I'd rather hear it from you." He turned on the stool to watch her.

"Now, I'll mix the blood with a stabilizing reagent, and the mixture will incubate at room temperature for two hours." She picked up a glass tube about the size of a large Tylenol capsule, then pipetted a clear fluid into the pellet along with the blood. Sealing the pellet with a tiny black cork, she then placed it in a stand.

"When will I get my results?"

"You won't. I mean, not until the study is closed and only if both you and your match chose to be notified. Again, if you'd read the consent form, you'd know that." She skirted around him, began picking up the debris, then turned to toss it into a red biohazard trash can. Stepping on the lid opener, she tugged off the gloves and tossed them in with the trash.

His gaze traveled up from her stilettos, along her calves, and up her legs where they disappeared beneath her skirt. "Your results go in my database and are used to prove my assay." When she turned again and tried to step around him, he caught her, hands at her waist, and pulled her in between his legs.

"Ethan," she admonished.

"Samantha," he replied in the same tone. "Now, what shall we do to pass the time while my blood incubates?"

"*We* will do nothing. *I*, however, will do some data analysis for another study." She tried to move from his grasp.

"I like you. I like kissing you. I like being with you."

"Ethan, I'm very busy."

"Yes, busy reducing the mysteries of love to numbers in a database when I'm trying to show you what romance is."

"Rom—"

He pressed his lips to hers, testing, tasting, gathering his own form of data. Attempting to replicate his experiment from Friday night. Her lips parted and her hands found their way to his thighs, settling there, their heat penetrating the fabric of his pants.

She tasted exactly as he'd remembered, and with the tightening in his groin, he knew he'd replicated the experiment. Perfectly. His methodology had proven their chemical reaction resulted in a hard-on of epic proportions.

She gripped his thighs and moaned into his mouth.

Skimming his hands along her ribs, he stopped just beneath her breasts. Swaying into him, she became pliant. *Sweet Jesus.* He'd better put a stop to this. A student or another professor could walk in any minute, and while the university didn't have a policy prohibiting fraternization among the faculty and staff, he was pretty sure the administration would frown on sexual activity on university property. Like lab countertops.

Hands back at her hips, he broke the kiss and pushed her away. "Samantha. Not here." Her eyes, hooded with desire, gazed back at him, as if she'd momentarily lost track of time and place. Her lips, wet and swollen from the kiss, parted. Her breasts rose and fell with each pant. God, she was the most beautiful thing he'd ever seen. That glazed look suddenly cleared, and she took a step back, glancing around as if to orient herself.

ATTEMPTING to gain some control over her erratic heartbeat, Sam took a deep breath. How did he do that? How did Ethan Quinn make her forget where she was and what she should—and shouldn't—be doing?

And made her want things she didn't typically want. Like hot, sweaty sex. On the countertop in her lab.

"You started it," she muttered. Her gaze darted to the bulge in the front of his pants, then lifted to his face. His warm brown eyes stared back.

Giving herself a mental shake, she said, "I almost forgot. You need to log on to this website and take the compatibility questionnaire." She handed him a card. "This card has your unique code and password. Once you've completed the questionnaire, hit submit. Your responses will automatically upload to my database with your unique code so I can match it to your blood-test results."

"Sam." Ethan shoved the card in his front pants pocket, then winced. "I don't need a blood test to prove we have chemistry. I feel it every time we're in a room together. Every time our eyes meet. And when we kiss—holy hell—it's like an atom bomb detonating."

Sam shook her head. She couldn't let this happen. She couldn't get tangled up with Ethan. Or anyone. She had her work. Her career. And she didn't plan to stick around Sterling University forever. Besides, now he was one of her research subjects.

While she might not be looking for a long-term relationship, she wasn't looking for a fling either—far from it. In fact, she wasn't looking for *anything* but advancing her career at the moment. "No."

"No?"

"No. Look, Ethan. I like you, and yes, we have chemistry, but it's purely physical."

"And?" He stepped closer, and she held up her hand.

"And, Sterling hired me to bring this assay to market, and that's what I have to focus my time and my attention on." It even sounded lame to her own ears.

Ethan chuckled. "Whatever helps you sleep at night, sweetheart."

He picked up his copy of the consent form then said, "I'll see you Wednesday." He grazed her lips with his, and she forced hers closed like he was trying to feed her liver and onions. This only elicited another chuckle from him. "See ya, Dr. Love."

She released a sigh as soon as he'd cleared her door.

That was one frustrating, sexy, hot-blooded male. And she needed to stay the hell away from him.

She'd buy him lunch on Wednesday, paying off her debt, then avoid him thereafter. Even in a small college town, that couldn't be too difficult, right?

5

—————

Ethan strode down the corridor to his office. He'd ducked into the men's room near Sam's lab and waited for … things … to deflate. Not an easy task, given the taste of Sam's mouth was still on his lips and tongue.

He stopped by his assistant's desk. Melinda handed him a stack of messages, three of which were from a helicopter parent of one of his students. She'd been upset over the grade he'd given her son on his paper on Thomas Hardy's women. He'd compared them to the Kardashians.

"Guess what?" Melinda interrupted his fantasy of telling the mom her son would never be the next Tom Wolf and that she should just give up.

"What?"

She handed him a stack of mail, a Cheshire Cat grin adorning her face. "I won the pool." At his confused frown, she continued, "You know, the one about who would date Dr. Love first?"

He rolled his eyes. "And how did you win?" He thought

taking Sam to Lake Ketchum and bypassing Dave's would be clandestine enough to avoid the gossip. Apparently not.

"Stan Gillespie saw you and Dr. Love walking out to the marina on Friday night. She was dressed up, and you had your hand on her back. That was a date, right?"

Ethan heaved a heavy sigh. "Clearly I don't keep you busy enough. Yes, it was a date." He took his stack of mail from her, shuffled through it. "I hope your bet was worth it."

"You bet it was. I won five hundred dollars."

"Five—Je-sus! You people really need to get a life." He shook his head and walked toward his office. Five hundred dollars over who'd be the first to take Samantha out. *Good Lord.*

He nodded to Frank Carson, the ancient contemporary-lit professor, as he passed, then unlocked his office door.

Once inside, he picked up the phone to call his mom. She'd relented on the possible job, and her interview with the Department of Social Sciences had been that morning.

"Hello."

"Hi, Mom. How'd the interview go?"

"Good, I think. It's been so long since I've had an interview, I have little to compare it to. But they said they'd let me know by the end of the week."

"And what did you think about the people you met?" That was just as important as them liking her.

"They were very nice. And Tiffany Hannon, the chair's executive assistant, is Marilee Hannon's daughter-in-law. You remember Marilee? You met her at your father's funeral. She works in the administrative offices of Sterling Granite."

"Yes, I remember her." Marilee liked to talk about her husband's gout—*ad nauseam.*

"Well, I'm glad you liked everyone." He was trying to

stay out of it, but he was sorely tempted to walk to the other side of the building and ask Tiffany if she thought his mother had a chance. "I'll come over for dinner tomorrow night."

"Good. I'll make that pork tenderloin you like so much. You know, the one with the mustard-bourbon glaze."

"Sounds good. Love you." He hung up the phone and sorted his mail, tossing the junk, stacking the academic journals for future reading, and opening the letters. One was from a literary journal, accepting his article on the economy and romance poets. Another was from his publisher. He was compiling and editing a book on nineteenth-century poetry.

The last one was from a headhunter. A prestigious university in Boston was in the market for a dean for their College of Arts and Sciences.

While he had a career goal of becoming a dean, he preferred to stay right here at Sterling.

Tossing the mail aside, his thoughts drifted back to the lovely professor and her theories on love. Or, to use her word, compatibility. He knew in his bones they were compatible. He just needed to prove his own theory to her. Everyone needed a little romance in their lives. Especially sexy college professors who thought it was overrated.

"I'M STUFFED," Delaney said, as she stretched out her legs on one of Sam's two sofas, a glass of plum wine in her hand.

Sam joined her on the opposite sofa. Who knew Asian-Southern fusion could be so good? In keeping with her alibi, they'd ordered takeout from Bubba Buddha and dined on egg rolls stuffed with turnip greens and pulled pork, egg-drop gumbo, spicy Hunan catfish, and buttermilk fried-chicken lo mein.

True to form, Delaney had pumped her for the details on her date with Ethan, including the toe-curling kisses. But Sam wasn't one to kiss and tell, no matter how much Delaney begged.

"You know, a really good friend would give her currently celibate friend some details. I've hit a dry spell, so I need to live vicariously through you."

Sam shook her head. "Let it go."

Throwing her head back in dramatic fashion, Delaney groaned. "You are one cruel doctor, Dr. Love." She tipped up her glass, draining it.

Unlike Sam, Delaney over-shared the intimate details of her love life—that is when she had one. Her last exploit involved a visiting chemistry professor, but that had fizzled like day-old soda.

Sitting up like she'd been prodded with a red hot poker Delaney said, "So! Ethan's in your study. How'd that happen?"

Sam lifted a shoulder, trying to appear nonchalant. "He asked me about my research and wanted to participate." She didn't say he considered it a challenge.

"Mm-hmm. And tell me, was there any hanky-panky in the lab after I left?"

Sam could feel the heat creep into her cheeks—one of the downfalls of being a fair-skinned redhead.

Delaney pointed, a big grin on her face. "There was! Do tell."

"What gave you that idea?"

"Oh, I don't know, maybe it's the nuclear reactor flush in your cheeks."

"It could be the wine." Sam ducked her head, hoping to hide the flush as it intensified.

"It could be, but in this case it's not."

"Fine. He kissed me." She waved her hand as if it were inconsequential when it was anything but.

"Oh, oh!" She leaned forward. "Was their groping involved?"

Sam recalled his hands sliding up her ribs, her hands gripping his thighs. "No. No groping."

"Well, darn. Maybe next time." Delaney poured another glass of wine and settled back on the sofa.

The doorbell rang.

"Who could that be?" Sam set her glass of wine on the table and made her way to the front door. Peering through the peephole, she saw a human, but she couldn't tell if it was male or female, holding a bouquet of the largest sunflowers she'd ever seen. Thinking they had the wrong house, she opened the door.

"Samantha Love?" the disembodied voice asked.

"Yes."

"These are for you." Hands shoved the vase of flowers at her.

"Um, thank you." Taking the vase, she watched as a young man ran down the steps back to his delivery truck.

Entering the house, she took the flowers to the coffee table.

"What's this?" Delaney touched the bright yellow petals. "Aren't they beautiful?!"

Finding the card amid the bright yellow petals, Sam opened it.

"Each kiss a heart-quake . . ." Lord Byron,
    Don Juan

I look forward to more heart-quakes.
Yours,
EQ

Delaney peered over her shoulder. "Look at you, Sam. You've got a boyfriend."

~

ETHAN WALKED alongside Sam back to campus after lunch at Bistro Café, heavy clouds providing a welcome respite from the sun, if not the humidity.

True to his word, he'd let her pay, even if it went against his upbringing. "Thank you for lunch." Ethan slipped Sam's arm through his.

She in turn disentangled herself, frowning. "Now we're even."

"Even?"

"Yes. For helping me with my car. And thank you for the flowers, by the way," Sam said, while he let her previous comment sit for a moment.

"You're welcome." He tried to take her hand, but again, she escaped.

Crossing her hands in front of her, she continued, her body language unmistakable. "Please don't send me anymore."

"Why? Are you allergic?"

"No." She shook her head. "It's just not necessary."

"Of course it's not *necessary*."

Sidestepping the newspaper stand in front of Dink's Corner Drugs, Ethan asked the question her earlier response evoked. "Why is it so important for you to 'pay your debt'?"

Sam shrugged. "I don't want to be beholden to anyone. I need to stand on my own two feet and rely on myself."

"And why is that?"

"It's what my parents always expected. I guess it stuck."

"Well, Dr. Love, did you know that giving a gift gives as much pleasure to the giver as to the receiver? That regularly performing good deeds increases longevity? And feeling indebted is not only unnecessary, but is often unwanted?" He glanced over at her to see if his words had had any effect. "So sit back and take it like a woman."

She smiled and shook her head. "Are you always this frustratingly obstinate?"

Sticking his hands in his pockets, he grinned. "Kettle? Meet pot."

"Point taken, but I have my reasons—"

"You don't like romance."

"It's difficult to like something you don't believe in."

"I don't know about that. I like the *idea* of Santa, even though I don't actually believe a corpulent bearded man delivers gifts to kids all over the world on Christmas Eve. Not to mention, I like the whole naughty-and-nice thing. Tell me, Dr. Love, are you naughty or nice?" He waggled his brows at her.

She stopped and looked at him. "You . . . I . . ." She threw up her hands in exasperation.

"Left you speechless." He grinned. "My work here is done."

THE FOLLOWING WEEK, Sam strode into her department chair's suite. "Oh, hi." Sam smiled at the woman sitting at the reception desk. She didn't recognize her. "You must be new. I don't believe we've met. I'm Samantha Love, I have a meeting with Dr. Carmichael."

The woman stuck out her hand. "I'm Margaret Quinn. I just started yesterday."

"Quinn?"

Before Sam could form a coherent question, Margaret replied, "Yes. Ethan is my son." There was no hiding a mother's pride in her voice. "And you're Dr. Love. My son has told me about you."

Uh-oh. She wondered what Ethan had told his mother about her. "Really?" She recalled that Ethan's father had passed away. She didn't know whether to bring it up or not. "Well, welcome to the department."

Mrs. Quinn appeared the quintessential Southern woman. Polite, nicely dressed, but unlike many of the ladies Sam had met, she wasn't made up to within an inch of her life. Her brown shoulder-length hair, similar in texture to Ethan's, was sparsely streaked with gray and worn in soft layers around her face. Ethan had clearly gotten his warm brown eyes from her.

"Dr. Love?" Tiffany asked. "Dr. Carmichael will see you now." She indicated the chair's office down the hall.

"Thanks, Tiffany. It was nice to meet you, Mrs. Quinn."

"Margaret, please."

"Margaret."

Sam walked through the hushed atmosphere of the chair's office. Just the sound of phones ringing in subtle tones, fingers flying across computer keyboards, and the hum of voices.

Dr. Carmichael wanted an update on her patent application. Growing his department required money, and getting a percentage of the royalties from her assay would go a long way toward making that goal a reality.

Unless a university waived their intellectual property interest in faculty inventions and discoveries, the university held the patent, took royalties from any license agreements it negotiated, and paid the inventor a portion of those royalties. Some of that money could also trickle down to the faculty member's home department.

NYU had had no interest in her compatibility assay, which is one of the reasons she'd left. Well, that, and Craig. Bringing an invention to market took money and time she didn't have. She wanted the support of a university with experience at filing patent applications and negotiating licensing deals. Even with the percentage of royalties the university would keep, it was worth it for her to bring her blood test to market.

Fifteen minutes later, pleased with the discussion, Sam left Dr. Carmichael's office then stopped short when she recognized a voice.

"Where would you like to go to lunch?" he asked.

"Oh, Ruby's is fine," his mother answered.

Her heart squeezed a little in her chest. He was taking his mother to lunch. How thoughtful was that?

She debated whether she should hide until Ethan left, then thought better of it. Continuing down the hall, she entered the reception area.

"Well, if it isn't Dr. Love," Ethan said, giving her an appreciative once-over.

"Dr. Quinn." She nodded, keeping things on a professional level.

"We were just going to lunch. Why don't you join us?"

Before she could refuse, his mother blurted, "Yes. Won't you?"

Quick, think of something. Lunch with Ethan twice in the same week would set a bad precedent. And with his mother, no less. "I, uh, I have an experiment running in my lab, and I need to get back." Okay, not a total lie. She did have his blood in the chemical analyzer.

"How long will it take? We'll wait," he prodded.

"Oh, I wouldn't want to keep you."

"It's no problem," his mother said.

Sam looked into Mrs. Quinn's sweet face and couldn't say no. *Crap!* "Okay, why don't I meet you at Ruby's in fifteen minutes?"

"Perfect." Ethan indicated his mother should precede him through the door. "It will probably take that long to get a table anyway." He winked as he passed.

Sam groaned. For all her no-nonsense science, she was a sucker for a sweet face. And Ethan's mother had it in spades.

Ethan had just directed his mother to the booth when he saw Sam walk through the door where a small crowd waited for a table.

Ruby's did a brisk lunch business during the week, especially when Ruby dished up her Thursday special, chicken and dumplings with fresh homemade biscuits, white acre peas, and peach cobbler.

He raised his hand, getting Sam's attention. As she made her way through the busy restaurant, he took a moment to appreciate the subtle sexy that was Sam. She'd abandoned her standard blouse and pencil skirt for a dress that fit like a glove, stopping just below the knee. Her red hair, which hung loose today, stood out against the cobalt-blue of her dress.

"Please." Indicating that Sam should slide into the

booth, he gave her no option but to sit next to him. He slid in beside her, their thighs bumping beneath the table.

"Hi, Ethan. Mrs. Quinn," the waitress greeted them as she approached their table.

"Mellie, how's your mom?" Mrs. Quinn asked.

"She's hanging in there, thank you for asking."

Mellie handed out menus and took their drink orders. Melanie Grooms had been in Ethan's class from first grade all the way through high school. She'd had dreams of moving to New York and auditioning for Broadway, but then her mother was diagnosed with MS, and being the only girl, Mellie felt it her obligation to stay behind and take care of her mother.

After she left to get their drinks, Ethan set aside his menu. He knew what he wanted—Ruby's Thursday special.

"Isn't this nice?" Mrs. Quinn said, gazing across the table at him and Sam.

"Very nice," Ethan replied, intentionally knocking his leg against Sam's.

When she glanced his way, he grinned. For some absurd reason, he liked yanking Sam's chain. For one thing, it was easy. For another, it was entertaining. She always appeared so buttoned-up. So in control. Except when he poked at her. He enjoyed getting a rise out of her.

And then, there were those kisses. Buttoned-up Sam quickly became unbuttoned Sam. And he liked unbuttoned Sam. A whole lot.

"Ethan tells me you study love."

She threw Ethan a look. "Oh, well, not love so much as relationships and compatibility."

"Love," his mother returned, matter-of-factly, and Ethan chuckled.

"We've had this discussion before, Mom. You'd have a

better chance getting Sherman to say the burning of Atlanta was an unfortunate accident than you would getting Samantha to say her research is on love."

Mellie returned to take their orders, postponing Samantha's inevitable rebuttal.

Orders placed, Ethan returned to the discussion. "Samantha doesn't believe in romance."

His mother joined the fray. "Oh, honey, romance is what makes relationships last. It's that hug for no reason. That cuddle when you first wake up in the morning. And that kiss good night before you fall asleep. It's what shows your partner that you're thinking about him or her. It's what made me fall in love with Ethan's father."

Seeing the melancholy expression on his mother's face made him regret his line of discussion.

"Ethan's father and I were married for almost forty years. And they were the happiest years of my life because we never let a day go by without making each other feel loved and appreciated."

Ethan waited for Sam's response.

"Mrs. Quinn—"

"Margaret."

"Margaret, my research doesn't negate the need for respect between partners. It simply provides a basis to find the *right* partner. And if you find the right partner, there's no need to spend money many people don't have on flowers and jewelry to keep that partner happy. Your chemistry tells you you're meant to be together."

"Honey, not to disparage your research, but chemistry doesn't mean much when you're both so sleep-deprived from your newborn child's upside-down sleeping schedule that you don't know which end is up. It's your husband's offer to get up with the baby even though he's got to go to work the next morning. It's when he takes you in his arms and sways to your favorite song, even after he's been on his feet all day. That's what love is. That's what makes for a happy relationship."

Ethan looked across the table at his mother's face. Memories of his father pulling his mother into his arms and dancing around the kitchen with her as she giggled like a schoolgirl swept through him.

Mellie returned with plates piled high with food and slid them across the table. Ethan frowned at Sam's salad. "You passed up Ruby's chicken and dumplings for a salad?"

She snorted. "Yeah. Delaney and I had Bubba Buddha's last night."

He chuckled. "Enough said."

Just as he took a big swig of his iced tea, his mom chimed in.

"Well, I may not agree with your theories, but I'm happy you're dating my son."

Oh shit. He coughed as the tea went down the wrong pipe. So much for subtle.

"YOU LOOK SHELL-SHOCKED," Delaney said, as she walked into Sam's lab. "What's up?"

"Nothing." She'd returned from lunch to evaluate her latest test results. "I, uh, I ran the latest blood I collected through my assay, and I have a match." Sam sat in front of her computer staring at the results on the screen. She'd checked and rechecked them, certain there must be a mistake. First, his mom's comment about them dating, and now this.

"Ooh, is it mine?" Delaney leaned against the lab counter, eager for the results.

"No. It's mine."

"Shut the front door!" She popped up like she'd just been goosed. "Who's the lucky guy? Or gal?"

"Subject 7645. Ethan Quinn." *Crap.* If only she could hit rewind. She shouldn't have disclosed his name.

"Ethan Quinn? You've got to be kidding me!" She came around the counter and gave Sam a nudge. "That's good isn't it? Isn't that good?" She bent over and studied Sam's face. "You don't look like that's good."

"It's not."

Straightening, hands on her hips, she continued, "Why isn't that good? I got some pretty hot vibes off you two the other day when he was in here."

Sam had looked at their compatibility questionnaires as well. Same results. Groaning, she buried her face in her hands. She didn't *want* a match. She didn't *need* a match. If Craig Sinclair had taught her anything, it was that she didn't need a man, and she certainly didn't want one. "Well, don't."

"Don't what?"

She turned and pointed her finger at Delaney. "Don't get any hot vibes off me and Ethan."

"Sister, I've got news for you, the hot vibes coming off you two could melt *Iceman*."

"Iceman?" Sam looked at Delaney in confusion.

"Yeah, you know, X-Men? Marvel Comics? Hunk Shawn Ashmore?"

Sam shook her head, clueless.

"You really need to get out more. And don't try to change the subject. Why is this a problem?" Delaney threw up her hands. "You're dating him."

"No. No, I'm not dating him." Sam wagged a finger in

Delaney's face. "And because it is. Because I don't *want* a man. Especially a man like Ethan Quinn."

"You mean a sexy man? A smart, educated man? A man that loves his momma but doesn't live with her? That kind of man?" She threw her hands up in the air again. "No. I mean, what woman in her right mind would want *that* kind of man?"

Sam rested her head in her hand and sighed. Why had she enrolled him in her study? Why had she told Delaney about the match? Now what? He'd opted to learn if he had any matches after the study closed. *Gah!*

Delaney placed her hand on Sam's shoulder. "Are you going to tell him?"

She sat up. "No. Absolutely not. The consent form tells participants they will not receive their results."

"Until the end of the study. Did he opt for that?"

"Yeah. He did." Unfortunately. *That* part of the consent form he read.

Delaney took a deep breath, then released it. "Okay, look. I know you're a scientist, and you need to do the ethical thing here, but the consent form doesn't say that you *can't* tell him before the end of the study. So, really, what harm could come of telling him you two are a match?"

What harm? Where should she start? Him thinking it's a tacit admission that she has feelings for him. Him thinking she's after an engagement ring and a white dress. Him believing they have a future together when they don't. Sterling was just a steppingstone in her career, and he clearly had deep roots in the community. Whereas she had shallow roots.

She was the rolling stone to his Rock of Gibraltar.

"Hey, wait a minute." Delaney pulled up a chair across from Sam. "If you believe in your science, doesn't it follow that you should believe he's your perfect histocompatible mate? And that, according to your research, histocompatible mates make the happiest relationships?"

Sam knew where Delaney was going with this, and she didn't like it. Not one bit. She closed her eyes against the reality of her situation then reopened them to see Delaney, deep in thought, now pacing the small confines of the lab.

"And if you don't believe he's your perfect mate, doesn't that bring into question your research? Your compatibility assay? Your reputation. Your very *career*?" Delaney stopped, looked Sam right in the eye. "Wouldn't that make you a hypocrite?"

6

Ethan threw out the first pitch, a slider, then removed his cap and scratched his head and, at the catcher's signal, adjusted for a change up.

The Sterling Nads faculty intramural team was playing Elberton Technical College in a rivalry match. Sterling won the last two, and the Elberton Exabytes were out for blood.

Two strikes, one more to go. He shot a glance over his left shoulder toward first base, where Nash guarded the bag. The runner's body language spoke volumes, and it said 'steal.' Ethan spun and whipped the ball to Nash, catching the runner unaware. Nash tagged him out to home-team applause.

As the sun slid below the horizon, players and fans alike breathed a sigh of relief. The heat this summer had been brutal, with only a few afternoon thunderstorms to provide relief. Maybe the predicted strong storm system that promised to dump record rains on the area would bring some relatively cooler temperatures.

In the meantime, Ethan had a batter to strike out.

Turning for the windup, a pair of sexy legs in shorts

caught his eye. The red ponytail was unmistakably Sam's. He watched her making her way up the stands and grinned.

He'd just started to wind up the pitch when she bent over to pick up something. The ball slipped, catching the batter on the ankle, sending him to first base.

"Damn!" *Get your head back in the game, Quinn, and stop ogling Dr. Love's behind.*

Stepping off the mound, he pretended to take a break. Pulling his cap lower over his eyes, he looked up into the stands again. In those shorts, a tank top, and sunglasses, Sam could have been at home at a pool party or on the lake. Thoughts of a refreshing swim led to thoughts of skinny-dipping, which lead to thoughts of—"Shake it off, man."

"Hey, Quinn, you gonna pitch or do we need to call in a reliever?" Rich Davis, the ump called from behind home plate, as the catcher rose.

Ethan flagged off his catcher and walked back to the mound with an uncharacteristic case of performance anxiety.

SAM FOLLOWED Delaney up the home-team bleachers toward the top, a perspiring diet soda in her hand. Damn, it was hot, even though the sun had already set.

Delaney selected a spot and took a seat, clapping her hands with a shout, "Let's go Nads!"

Sam rolled her eyes. "The Nads? Geez, whose idea was that?" Opening a bag of peanuts, the only reasonably healthy thing she could find at the concession stand, she offered one to Delaney.

"Probably Dr. Trotter's—he likes to talk about man bits."

Delaney pried open the peanut, removed the nuts, and tossed the shell.

Sam took a sip of her soda and found Ethan on the pitcher's mound where he'd just hit the batter.

"That's the second batter Ethan's hit since we got here. Wonder what's up." Delaney leaned back, elbows on the empty bleacher behind her. "What better way to spend an evening than watching a bunch of hot guys in tight pants flex their muscles and display their athletic prowess?"

"Is that all you ever think about?"

"No. I also think about hot guys in swim trunks. Hot guys in wet T-shirts. Oh, and hot guys in nothing."

Sam laughed and shook her head. If only she could be that open and honest about sex. Setting aside her cup, she tilted her head to admire Ethan's backside. Delaney was onto something with the whole tight-pants thing. Ethan filled out his pair nicely.

But fine behind aside, she'd vowed to avoid him. She didn't have a poker face, so keeping her secret from Ethan was going to be tough enough without running into him on campus. And she would not get tangled up with him and his romantic notions. The best thing for both of them was to steer clear of one another.

Feelings of guilt flickered through her. As a scientist, she'd promised the results to those who'd opted for them. It was part of her promise to those who took the time to participate in her study. Ethan Quinn was no different than her other subjects.

She snorted. Right. If you didn't count the fact that their chemistry was off the charts.

"Swing batter, batter, batter!" Delaney hollered.

After a pop fly, Ethan struck out the next batter and headed for the dugout. Moments later he came out, bat in hand, took a few warm-up swings, then approached the batter's box.

"Ethan's one of our best hitters," Delaney said, around a bite of soft pretzel liberally slathered with mustard. "He pitched for Sterling in undergrad." She gestured with her soda cup to another batter warming up outside the dugout. "And Nash, first baseman and Sterling's hunky football coach, is right behind him."

Ethan stepped into the batter's box, got in position, and swung.

"Ste-rike!" the ump called.

"Come on, Quinn," Nash called.

The pitcher released the next pitch, and PING! Ethan threw the bat aside, loping to first base as he watched the ball sail over the fence. Home run.

She had to admit a little pride in that.

His teammates waited at home plate, where high-fives, fist-bumps, and ass-pats welcomed him. Just shy of the dugout, he turned in Sam's direction, saluting her with his cap and a big smile. Heads turned in her direction as a flush crept up her neck.

Delaney gave her a shoulder-nudge. "Aww. It must be love."

ETHAN SLUNG his bag over his shoulder and headed in the direction of Sam and Delaney. Delaney smiled and laughed with the third baseman, Steve Kirkland from engineering, while Sam looked . . . uncomfortable.

"Sam," Ethan said, as he sidled up next to her. "Did you enjoy the game?" They'd won again by two runs in the bottom of the ninth.

"Yeah. You, uh, you looked pretty good out there."

"*Pretty* good?" He shook his head and laughed. "Well, all right then. Way to stroke a man's ego." Steve pulled Delaney away to introduce her to his kid brother. "Want to go grab something to eat? A few of us are heading over to Ruby's."

"Oh. Thanks, but no. I promised Delaney we'd go to that new pub in Carlyle." She frowned over her shoulder at Delaney as she flirted with Steve.

Sam's hair had curled around her face in the humidity, and she had a fine sheen of perspiration on her arms and chest. He wondered what it would be like to shake loose that ponytail and make her sweat for a different reason. *Head. Gutter. Out.*

Disappointed, he said, "Maybe next time then. Hey, when do you think you'll have the results from your love assay?"

"Compatibility—"

"Whatever."

"Soon. I've been distracted in my search for another grad assistant. But you won't know the results until the study closes. You'd know that—"

"Yeah, yeah, if I'd read the consent form," he finished with a grin.

"Oh, Ethan!" He winced at the sound of his name and turned.

"Hi, Jackie."

Jackie Ledbetter winnowed in between him and Sam. "You were awesome tonight!" She laid her hand on his forearm. "That home run! And that catch!" she gushed.

A single mom, Jackie was on the hunt for a new daddy for her five-year-old son. Little Jack was a good kid as far as he could tell, but he had no desire to become Jackie's next prey, *er*, husband.

Jackie was a firm believer in the idiom, 'The higher the hair, the closer to God,' and wore enough goop on her face to rival the rock band Kiss.

"Awesome, huh?" Ethan grinned over Jackie's head into Sam's eyes. "Some people thought my performance tonight only pretty good."

"Pretty good? Why, who on earth would say that?" Jackie asked in astonishment.

At least *someone* liked to stroke his ego. He flashed a grin at Sam, who narrowed her eyes in return.

Remembering his manners, he introduced the two women.

"Love." Jackie tapped her chin in thought. Her eyes widened, and she pointed her finger at Sam. "You're the one with that blood test. The one that tells people who their soul mates are. I saw your flier in Dink's Corner Drugs the other day."

Ethan glanced at Sam in time to see her cringe.

"I wouldn't say soul—"

"Sign me up." She nudged Ethan, as she stuck out her arm as if ready for a blood draw.

"Oh, well . . ."

Jackie patted Ethan on the belly and smiled up at him. "You never know, Ethan, maybe we're soul mates."

Now it was Ethan's turn to cringe.

"Just, uh, call the number on the flier and schedule an appointment to come to my lab."

Jackie clapped her hands and looked back at Ethan.

Oh, joy.

"Good night, Ethan," Sam said.

The last thing he saw over Jackie's high hair was Sam grabbing a reluctant Delaney by the arm and hauling her toward the parking lot.

To say Sam dreaded her next research subject like she dreaded a root canal would be putting it mildly. No sooner had she taken the consent form out of the file when in walked Jackie Ledbetter of the high hair.

"Well, hi there, Dr. Love." Her cheerful expression was all Southern charm, but Sam felt the woman's scrutiny of her like an opponent assessing her rival.

"Ms. Ledbetter." Sam nodded.

Jackie giggled and waved her hand. "Oh, please. Call me Jackie."

Sam hadn't seen that much hairspray since, well, since she saw the *Hairspray* revival on Broadway.

"Well, Jackie, I'll review the consent form with you, and then I'd like you to read it thoroughly and ask me any questions you might have before signing it."

While Jackie read over the document, Sam finished setting up for the blood test.

"Wait—you mean I won't find out if I have any matches?" Jackie asked, looking up from the document, the distress clear in her voice. "What's the point then?"

"You will learn if you have any matches once the study is closed, and only if your match also consented to it."

A scowl marred Jackie's make-up-slathered face. "When will the study be closed? I mean, I'm not getting any younger here."

"The study will likely close within the next month or two."

"Oh, good! I'm hoping for Ethan. Ooh, or Nash Taylor. Has he signed up for your study?"

"I can't say."

"Oh, right. That would violate the psychologist-patient privilege."

Sam didn't bother to explain that there was no psychologist-patient privilege involved in this context. Just her promise to her subjects not to reveal any confidential information about them without their express consent.

Jackie scrawled her signature on the document and handed it back to Sam.

As Sam prepared her finger for the stick, Jackie continued, "I'm a perfect match for Ethan. He just doesn't see it. Yet." She winked at Sam, and the sharp knife of jealousy stabbed Sam in the heart just as she jabbed Jackie's finger with the lancet. Just a *tad* harder than was necessary.

"Ouch! That hurt!"

"Sorry. Didn't I mention that part?"

Jackie grimaced, but continued, "Even so, I'm not opposed to Nash either."

After filling the collection tube, Sam wrapped a Band-Aid around her finger as Jackie prattled on. "I would never do to Ethan what his last girlfriend did to him."

Sam frowned but took the bait. "What did his last girlfriend do to him?"

"Well, rumor was that he popped the question, and not only did she say no, she left for another job in New York." She paused. "Or was it D.C.? Anyway, somewhere up north. She was always a little too high and mighty if you ask me. North Georgia was never going to be her home. Too . . . what did she say? Oh, yes, too backward." Jackie snorted in contempt and rambled on.

Sterling wasn't exactly New York City, but Sam had known that coming into this job. When she left, it would have nothing to do with the size or sophistication of Sterling. It would have everything to do with taking the next step in her academic career.

"Don't you agree?" Jackie asked her.

"Hmm?"

"I said, men often don't know what's good for them. They need to be taken in hand by a good woman."

She didn't think Ethan, or most other men she knew, wanted to be "taken in hand." That is, unless you were talking about foreplay. "Oh. Well. I wouldn't say that. But my research shows that couples whose MHC-P1 are on opposite ends of the spectrum—indicating their MHC genes are dissimilar—not only have healthier, more productive children, but they also have longer, happier relationships."

Jackie blinked. "I don't know what you just said, but," she shrugged, "if it means Ethan is my match, I don't care."

SAM HAD BEEN AVOIDING HIM. His phone calls and messages had gone ignored. He didn't know what he'd done or said, but as his father had taught him, apologies worked wonders. Especially when accompanied by flowers.

Determined to confront her, he checked her office hours on the university's digital directory. Flowers in hand, he strode toward her wing of the building.

Hearing a conversation, he stood outside the door waiting. He hadn't waited long when a student with a backpack that looked as if it were filled with bricks instead of books nearly collided with him.

He knocked on her door.

"Come in."

He stuck the flowers in the doorway. "Delivery for Dr. Love."

When he stepped into her office, Sam looked up and the smile she wore froze. "Ethan."

"So, you do remember my name."

"What does that mean?" She set her pen down and folded her hands on top of the desk.

"Well, you've been avoiding my phone calls and text messages as if I were a telemarketer."

"I've just been," she waved her hand, "busy."

"Not buying it. Why are you avoiding me?" He scrubbed his hands through his hair. "Was it something I said? Something I did?"

Appearing uncomfortable, she could barely look him in the eye.

She shrugged. "What reason would I have to avoid you? Or to seek you out? We're colleagues. Either we see each other on campus or around town or we don't."

"Colleagues is it? Do you often have your colleagues' tongues down your throat?"

"That was a mistake."

"Well, that's news to me."

"Ethan, I can't have a relationship with you."

"Can't, or won't?"

"Both."

"I think I at least deserve to know why."

Picking up her pen again, she gripped it like a lifeline. "We've talked about this before. I need to focus. On my career. On my patent. On my goals."

"You know, your career and our relationship aren't mutually exclusive. Couples the world over manage to have successful careers and relationships—at the same time."

She narrowed her eyes. "Couples? Ethan, we aren't a couple."

"Not yet. But we could be if you would just give it a

chance." He had a sick feeling in the pit of his stomach. When she didn't respond, he prodded, "What are you afraid of?"

Biting her lip, she looked away. "Who says I'm afraid?"

"It's written all over your face." Seeing her expression made him ache for her, and made him wonder if Craig had put that fear there.

Her expression turned obstinate, and he knew nothing he could say would change her mind. "So this is it then?"

"I'm sorry if I hurt you, but yes, this can't go any further. I'm just trying to be fair to you."

"How about you? Are you being fair to yourself?"

Sam rose from her chair, hands on her desk. "I have to go. I have a potential subject coming to my lab in ten minutes."

Ethan strode over to the desk and laid the flowers on top of her papers. "Well, I hope you and your career are very happy together."

7

"**S**evere weather is headed our way later tonight," the local weatherman said. "Be sure to have your weather radio next to you and plenty of candles or a flashlight handy."

"Great," Sam muttered, as she sat on her sofa with a Lean Cuisine in her hands.

"Expect high winds, heavy rain, potential flash floods, and possible hail." As if to punctuate his words, a low rumble of thunder rolled across the area. "Stay tuned for updates throughout the evening."

Sam hated storms. Living in New York the last few years, she'd dealt with snowstorms—even some thunder snow—but nothing like the violent summer storms here. This was something new and frightening.

Finishing up her dinner, she tried to settle her nerves as a crack of thunder shook the house, rattling the dishes in the cabinet. Lightning followed close on its heels, along with another loud boom.

Between breaking up with Ethan and now this, she was a bundle of nerves. She snorted. Breaking up? Where had that come from? How do you break up with someone you never had a relationship with in the first place?

She hadn't lied when she'd told Ethan she needed to focus on her career. But that wasn't the only reason for discouraging his interest in her.

He'd asked her what she was so afraid of.

Disappointment. Not hers. His.

Relationships meant intimacy—sex. Not one of her talents, as Craig had so callously informed her when he'd dumped her. If she couldn't please someone as dispassionate as Craig, how could she ever hope to please someone as passionate as Ethan?

Thunder rumbled overhead, closer than before. She needed a distraction—from Ethan, and from Mother Nature's fury.

Until her new grad assistant started, she had papers she should grade, but what she needed was a good book. Too bad she didn't have one of Delaney's fluffy romance novels. Going to her bookshelves, she selected a mystery. It would have to do. As long as it didn't start with 'It was a dark and stormy night.'

She'd barely opened the book when her cell phone rang. "Hi, Delaney."

"You okay?"

"So far," she said with a shaky laugh.

"Listen, I can come over if you'd like."

"No. Don't be silly. You don't want to come out in this." KA-BAM! "Holy shit!"

"I know, right?" Delaney commiserated. "I grew up in Tornado Alley, so I'm used to this, but if you get scared, just call me and I'll come over."

"Thanks, but I'll be fine. I'm a big girl." Sort of.

"If you change your mind, you know where to find me."

She ended the call, released a shaky sigh, then picked up her book. Just as she opened to the first page, the lights flickered, then went out.

ETHAN PACED HIS LIVING ROOM, while the weather alert scrolled across the television screen. He'd persuaded his mother to stay at her neighbors so she wouldn't be alone. Now his concern turned to Sam.

The storm had the potential for downed trees and power lines, not to mention flash flooding. He tried to call Sam but got no answer.

When the meteorologist came on and said residents of Georgetown Square should take cover, Ethan made up his mind. After grabbing his chainsaw, he pulled on his rain jacket, picked up his keys, and he headed for his car.

The heavy rain and wind made the drive across town treacherous. When he'd arrived, Sam's neighborhood was pitch black. In his headlights, he could see some limbs and other debris strewn along the street, and finding Sam's townhouse in the dark was no easy task.

Placing a ball cap on his head, he pulled the hood over his head before dashing through the blinding rain. Hail the size of marbles began to pelt him. "Ow! Jesus." He reached the front door and hammered with his fist, afraid otherwise she wouldn't be able to hear him over the onslaught.

The door flew open. "Ethan!" Then Sam wrapped herself around him like kudzu. "I'm soaked," he said, as he wrapped his hands around her waist.

"I don't care." She clung to him, even as he carried her into the dark house.

"Why on earth don't you have any lights?"

"The power's out."

"I know that. I mean where's your flashlight? Candles?"

"I, uh . . . probably still in those boxes I haven't unpacked." She gestured toward the dining room.

"Jesus, Sam." He set her away from him and shed his jacket. Pulling his phone out of his back pocket, he found the flashlight app and turned it on. She looked like she'd just walked out of a horror movie, fear written all over her face. "Where is your phone? I tried to call you."

"Battery died and I couldn't charge it."

Lightning flickered and Sam winced. He wrapped his arms around her and she fell into his embrace. "How? Why did you come? You shouldn't have been out in this. It's too dangerous."

He released her, and she stepped back. "I was worried about you. You're trembling."

"I don't like storms."

In the dim light of his phone, he could see she was wearing some sort of pajama bottoms and a T-shirt that read, IF LOVE IS THE ANSWER, WHAT WAS THE QUESTION? Her hair was pulled up in a messy ponytail, and her feet were bare. She'd look adorable if she weren't so scared.

"Come on." He took her hand and pulled her into the living room. "Do you have anything to drink?"

"There's a bottle of Scotch in the cabinet by the fridge."

"Good. You sit here and I'll be right back." He left her on the sofa and made his way to the kitchen. He found the bottle of Scotch then, after some searching, came up with two glasses.

Thunder shook the house as a gust of wind blew something against the window. From the sound of it, hail still clattered against the roof.

Pouring two fingers of Scotch into each glass, he carried

them into the living room. "Here." He placed the glass in her hand and settled down next to her on the sofa. Wrapping a hand around her waist, he pulled her next to him. "Drink up. It'll take the edge off." He tapped his glass to hers. "To Mother Nature's fury."

SAM LIFTED the glass to her lips and drank a healthy serving, coughing as the liquid burned its way down her throat. But, after a moment, the heat it delivered relaxed her.

When she'd opened the door and saw Ethan standing there, she'd never been so glad to see anyone in her life.

Lightning flickered in the darkened house like a strobe light, illuminating Ethan's strong profile, casting his face in eerie light and shadow. He'd come through this hellish storm to check on her, even after the way she'd treated him. She didn't know what to say, so she simply said, "Thank you."

"For what?"

"For doing something stupid like driving in this storm to make sure I was okay."

He chuckled. "You're welcome, even if you think it was stupid."

She snuggled closer, enjoying the feel of his warmth and the security of his arms.

"Feeling better?"

She nodded against his shoulder.

"Good." He pressed a kiss to the top of her head, and her heart did a slow roll in her chest at the tender gesture.

The wind shook the house as if trying to knock it from its foundations, while the hail did its best to pierce the roof shingles. But none of it mattered. Ethan made soothing circles on her bare arm as they polished off their drinks.

"Why are you so afraid of storms?"

"The storms here in Georgia are so violent. Unlike any storms I've ever experienced."

"You're safe. I won't let anything happen to you."

How soothing those words were. To know someone had your back.

Suddenly exhausted, she closed her eyes and nodded off for a moment.

"Hey." Ethan took the glass from her hand and set it on the coffee table. "Let's get you to bed."

Too tired to resist, she let him pull her to her feet, then he scooped her up and carried her up the stairs. She knew she should resist. In her Scotch-, fear-, and fatigue-fogged mind, she knew his game. Rescue frightened damsel in distress, then said rescued damsel would be so grateful she'd take him to bed. Only to have him end up dissatisfied. Still, she couldn't muster enough indignation.

He placed her in bed and pulled the covers up before kissing her forehead. "Good night, Sam. Sleep well."

Her eyes flew open. "You're leaving?"

"I'm not leaving you alone. I'll just be downstairs."

"But . . . don't go." She grabbed his hand. "Don't leave me up here alone."

"SHH. I'LL STAY." The fear in her voice broke his heart.

He laid down on top of the covers next to her and pulled her into his arms. As if the covers would be a barrier to her soft, warm body—and his almost painful need for her.

She snuggled against him, her breath against his neck. *Sweet Jesus.* Spending the night here would be pure torture.

"Ethan, why did you come here tonight?" The wind blew something against the window, and she flinched.

"Because I was worried about you."

She lifted herself up onto one elbow, and he felt her gaze on his face in the pitch darkness. "But, after everything I said—"

"Doesn't matter. When you care about someone, you want to help them. Protect them. No matter what."

"You care about me?" she whispered.

"I thought that was evident."

"I thought all that was just to prove a point."

"And that point being?"

"That flowers, candlelight dinners, and coming to my rescue—romantic gestures—would make me fall for you."

"Is it working?" He held his breath waiting for her answer.

After what seemed like an eternity, she finally said, "Yes."

"Thank God." He rolled her over and took her mouth with his. One hand fisted in his shirt while the other hand tangled in his hair. *Sweet. So damned sweet.* His tongue danced with hers, their breath mingling, converging. Deepening the kiss, he cupped her face, holding her there so he could drink his fill of her mouth.

Changing the angle, he slid his hand along her neck, and she sighed into his mouth. Continuing his exploration, his fingers skimmed her shoulder, traveling down her arm to where she was still grasping his shirt. From there, he found her hips and pressed her against him so she could feel the heat of his erection, groaning when their bodies made contact.

Her fisted hand pushed against his chest. "Wait."

"I'M NOT GOOD AT THIS," she panted.

With nothing more than the gentle pressure she applied against him, he withdrew, giving her space to think. To confess.

God, she wanted him. With every fiber of her being. Every nerve ending in her body was attuned to him. To his touch. His kiss. His heat. But, she needed him to understand. To know what he was getting. Or in this case, what he wasn't.

"Good at what?"

"This." She gestured between the two of them.

"Kissing? Oh, I beg to differ."

"No." She cleared her throat. "Sex."

"First, unless they've changed the rules, we're currently not having sex. Second, why would you say that?"

"Look." She sat up, shoving her hair out of her face. "Just because my parents are world-famous sex therapists doesn't mean—you know—I'm some kind of expert in the bedroom."

He took her shoulders, looked into her eyes. "Sam, this isn't some sort of competition. You're not being graded or anything."

"I just don't want you to have any expectations."

"Sam?" His finger drifted down her cheek to her mouth.

"Yes?"

"Shut up and let me make love to you."

His reassuring gaze never left her eyes as he patiently waited for response. She knew if she said no, he'd accept it and not pressure her. That alone made her want him all the more. "Yes." She turned, took his finger into her mouth, eliciting a caveman-like growl.

Dragging his finger from her mouth, he replaced it with his tongue, while the wet finger found her pebbled nipple through her shirt. Arching into him, she gasped. Electric. His touch sparked lust, greed, wantonness.

His mouth followed his finger as he captured her nipple through her T-shirt.

"Naked," she gasped as she tugged on his shirt hem. "I want you naked."

He chuckled low in his throat, and she felt it against her breast. Sitting up, he yanked the offending shirt over his head and tossed it behind him. Then made short work of her own T-shirt. When he laid back down, she hissed at the searing contact of skin against skin. Ten atomic bombs couldn't create this much heat.

Greed took over her hands. She wanted to touch every inch of his skin. His stomach quivered as her hand glided over him. The hard ridges of his abs, the smattering of hair on his chest, fueled a desire she never knew possible. Slipping lower, her hand encountered his erection, and she stroked it through his jeans.

He grabbed her wrist, groaning. "Slow down, sweetheart, or I won't last long. First things first."

Bringing her hand to his mouth, he kissed her wrist, then her palm, before releasing her. Settling her back against the bed, he lathed one nipple with his hot tongue, sending fire through her already-melting veins. Showing the same attention to her other breast, his hand grazed her bare stomach before slipping beneath her pajama bottoms.

She'd already almost reached the pinnacle, and with one touch she splintered into a million pieces.

HE KISSED HER TEMPLE, waiting until the last tremor dissipated. "How are you doing, sweetheart?"

"Good. I'm really . . ." she sighed, "good."

Cupping the back of his head, she lifted her mouth to his, biting his bottom lip. Her other hand was busy popping the button on his fly before unzipping his jeans. Plunging her hand in, she wrapped her fingers around him, making him draw in a breath.

Gritting his teeth, he let her explore him until he couldn't take anymore. Rising, he grabbed his wallet out of his pocket and pulled out a foil packet then dropped his jeans to the floor. He feared this wouldn't last long.

Rolling on the condom, he knelt on the bed and slid her pajama bottoms off. On the way back up, he grazed between her thighs with his fingertips, stirred by the moan that escaped her, and gratified by her waiting arms when he settled himself between those silky legs.

Positioning himself above her, he entered her in one long, slow glide. Holding himself in check, he reveled in the feel of her. Taking her mouth, he began to move with unhurried thrusts, getting to know what she liked. She wrapped her legs around his backside and arched to meet him.

"Ethan," she breathed, as her fingernails clawed at his back.

"I've got you, sweetheart." He picked up the pace, meeting her thrust-for-thrust, driving them higher and higher. The howl of the wind, the rumble of thunder, and the relentless onslaught of the rain faded into the background. Only the sound of their labored breathing, the moans of their mutual pleasure, filled the room.

With one last deep thrust, his soul tore in two, and when the pieces reunited, a part of hers was intertwined.

8

———————

Shattered was the first word that came to mind, transcendent the second.

"Sweetheart, why would you ever think you weren't any good at sex?" She lay curled up against his side, while his hand made gentle circles on her back.

She shrugged, the only movement she had the energy for. She didn't want to tell him that Craig had called her frigid.

He nudged her. Sighing, she finally responded. "Let's just say my past, um, partners, said I wasn't passionate."

"Well, then they must have been doing it wrong."

She giggled. He had that way about him. He shot through all her insecurities and made her laugh.

Disentangling himself, he propped himself up on one elbow and looked down into her face. "If you were any more passionate, the sheets would have caught fire."

She felt the flush creep up her chest and into her face. Ducking her head against his arm, she shook it.

Rolling her unto her back, he kissed her so sweet and slow, she felt her bones dissolve. Retreating a millimeter, he spoke against her lips, "That was, without a doubt, the best experience of my life. Not just sex. Experience."

Wide-eyed, she gazed into his face, as her heart filled with . . . something. "Me, too." Chalking it up to an oxytocin overload, she covered by asking if he was hungry.

Kissing her nose, he said, "Starved!"

"I think I can scare up some cheese and crackers, maybe a bottle of Pinot."

"A meal fit for a king," Ethan exclaimed. "Be right back." Sam could just make out his silhouette as he headed for the bathroom, and what a silhouette it was.

As soon as he returned, he turned on the flashlight app on his smartphone and shrugged into his jeans, sans shirt and shoes, while she wrapped herself in a silk robe, tying it at the waist.

Leading the way to the stairs, Ethan said, "Careful." Taking her hand, he guided her down the dimly lit staircase.

After laying out the crackers, cheese, some olives, and sliced prosciutto, ravenous, they fell upon it like it was manna from Heaven.

She'd unearthed a scented candle that Delaney had given her as a housewarming gift, so they ate by candlelight at the dining-room table. Though it still rained buckets outside, the storm had expended most of its energy, leaving behind only the occasional flicker of lightning and distant rumble of thunder.

Around a bite of provolone, Ethan asked, "Why the love assay?"

"Compatibility."

He winked. "Tomato, tomahto."

Rolling her eyes, she considered his question a moment because, honestly, she didn't know if she had an answer. It was really something she'd stumbled upon in her dissertation research about what makes some marriages or relation-ships last, and others not so much.

"My parents divorced when I was fifteen. And while they remain professional partners to this day, I always wondered why they couldn't stay married."

"Wait. Your parents, world-renowned sex therapists, aren't married?"

"No. They've kept it very quiet. They insist that they're an inseparable team when it comes to faculty positions. They still work together every day, write articles and books, even live together, but they're divorced. They see other people from time to time, but neither one has been in a rela-tionship."

Ethan scratched his chin, the sound of the day-old scruff sending delicious little shivers down her spine. "Huh."

"Yeah, I know. Weird." She sighed, took a sip of her wine, then continued. "So, I guess that's why my research took the turn it did." She lifted a shoulder. "Call it intellectual curiosity."

Ethan reached out and laid a big, warm hand over hers. "Or the little girl inside the woman trying to understand why her mom and dad don't love each other anymore."

Their divorce had always bothered her more than she'd let on. If two people so seemingly suited for one another, with identical interests, couldn't stay married, what hope did any couple have? Then there were Ethan's parents, whose marriage ended tragically. What was the formula for a long, happy marriage? To her mind, it all came down to chemistry.

But she began to wonder if Ethan, and his parents, weren't onto something. Her parents had the same profes-sions, the same goals, the same tastes in music and art, food and wine, yet their marriage had failed. Was it simply because they didn't believe in romance? Because they took each other for granted? Would chocolates and flowers, a tender gesture, or a kind word have made a difference?

Confused and uncertain, she chose to change the subject. "Your turn. Why literature?"

∼

"Nice deflection, Dr. Love."

"Guilty as charged." A soft smile lifted the corners of that delectable mouth. "But I really want to know," she finished softly.

"My dad loved reading but never had the money to pursue an education. It was his love of reading that made me decide to study literature." He topped a cracker with a slice of prosciutto and a piece of cheese, handing it to her.

"When I was too young to read, he would read *Oliver Twist*, *Robinson Crusoe*, or *Gulliver's Travels* to me at bedtime. When I was older, we'd read books like *A Tale of Two Cities*, *Tom Sawyer*, and *Huck Finn*, and we'd discuss them at dinner. Much to my sister's dismay." He chuckled, remembering Charlotte's protests.

She popped an olive into her mouth. "And your mom? Was she a big reader?"

"She loved Austen and Brontë, but she didn't venture far from romantic fiction."

"How old was your father when he died?"

"Sixty-four."

"Young."

"Too young." And it was his fault.

"You said it was a heart attack."

"Yeah." He scrubbed a hand over his face. How did they wind up talking about this?

"You don't have to talk about it if you don't want to."

She'd shared her sexual insecurities with him. Maybe he should share his feelings of guilt with her. "We were fishing out on Lake Ketchum. I'd talked him into it. He said he wasn't feeling well, but he'd been working a lot at the granite quarry, and I thought he just needed some fresh air and relaxation. Turned out I was wrong. What he'd needed was a trip to the hospital."

She stroked his cheek with her hand. "You couldn't have known that."

"I couldn't save him," he whispered. "No matter how long I did CPR, I couldn't keep him alive."

"Oh, Ethan." Sam rose from the table and knelt by his chair, her hands resting on his thighs. "You did everything you could. I'm sure your mom knows that. And you should, too."

Intellectually, he knew she was right. But, emotionally . . . well, that was another matter.

God, she was beautiful on her knees looking up at him, her eyes soft with compassion.

Draining the last of the wine from his glass, he rose and lifted her to her feet. Leaning over, he blew out the candle. Safety first. Then pulled her along behind him.

"Where are we going?"

"Bedroom."

"Wait."

"For what?" He stopped short, and she bumped into him in the dark.

"This." She grabbed his face and pulled his mouth down to hers, where she proceeded to lick and nip him like he was an ice cream cone.

Turning so that her back was to the stairs, he lowered her until she sat on the third step, and opening her robe, he proceeded to do the same to her. All the way down her sexy body until he reached her pearly gates.

"Talk about nice deflection," Sam said later—much later —as Ethan drew her up against him so they were spooning.

He chuckled, his breath tickling the back of her neck. "I aim to please, Dr. Love."

"Thank you. Again."

"Well, you don't have to thank me for the orgasms. That's just awkward."

She snorted. "I'm thanking you again for driving through the storm to see if I was okay."

"Oh. That." He kissed her neck. "You're safe, Dr. Love. Get some sleep." His arms tightened around her.

Should she tell him about the results? she wondered. No. Then he'd think she was after more than just sex.

That's what this was, right? Just sex? And what amazing sex it was! She wasn't frigid after all. Nor was she sexually unresponsive. She'd discovered her sexual mojo. And it felt . . . awesome!

Problem was, she may have discovered something else, too. Romance.

The next morning, Ethan surveyed the damage from Sam's living-room window. The beautiful tree-lined neighborhood had taken quite a hit. He took a sip from the coffee he'd managed to brew on Sam's gas range. His phone buzzed in his back pocket. Checking it, he saw a text from his mom saying all was well.

The power in the area was still out and likely would be for some time, and the house was already getting stuffy without AC.

It had taken every ounce of willpower to crawl out of Sam's bed so he could check on things. What happened between them last night had left him shaken. Off kilter. Their union had touched something deep inside his soul. Something inexplicable. He ran a palm down his face. And talking about his dad; well, that had been surprisingly . . . cathartic.

He'd gotten little sleep last night. And neither had Sam. Not because of the storm outside, but because of the storm inside. Her bedroom to be exact. Oh, and the staircase on their way back from the kitchen after their late-night snack. They'd burned a lot of calories last night.

It was early yet, and Sam hadn't stirred. He'd let her sleep.

The tree limb lying across her driveway would require a chainsaw to clear. Good thing he'd tossed his in the trunk of his car just in case. He'd thought he might need it to just get to her house last night. But now it would come in handy.

Finishing up the coffee, he set the cup in the kitchen sink and headed out just as the rip of a chainsaw down the street broke the post-storm silence.

SAM SIGHED as memories drifted across her consciousness. Ethan carrying her up the stairs, placing her in bed . . . then . . . nirvana. She sat up with a start.

The bed was empty. The pillow next to her revealed an indentation from where Ethan had slept. Alone in her bed, she didn't know how she felt about last night.

Physically, she was loose, relaxed. And satisfied. Most-definitely satisfied. All thanks to Ethan and the flood of the hormone DHEA in her system.

Before she could give her emotions more than a cursory analysis, the growl of a chainsaw ripped through the morning. Throwing back the covers, she drew on her robe as she walked over to the front window. Ethan stood, chainsaw in hand, arm muscles flexing, as the machine bit into wood. The limb was huge! Almost the size of a tree. And where had Ethan found the chainsaw? Certainly not in her tool-barren garage.

Grabbing a pair of jeans and a T-shirt, she dressed in a rush, brushed her teeth, and de-snarled her hair before pulling it up into a messy bun. Taking in her kiss-swollen mouth, her radiant complexion, and her silly smile, she high-fived herself in the mirror with a giggle.

As she headed down the stairs, the aroma of coffee had her detouring to the kitchen. Bless him, Ethan had made coffee. Cup in hand, she moved to the front window. Brow furrowed in concentration, Ethan attacked the downed limb with the skill of a lumberjack.

Thank goodness she'd parked her car in the garage, otherwise it would've been toast. On the other hand, if the tree limb *had* flattened it, she'd have a new car. Sighing at the injustice, she polished off the last of her coffee then went out to help.

Ethan looked up as she walked down the front steps. He shut off the chainsaw and lifted the safety glasses from his eyes. "Morning."

Damn, but he was a beautiful man! "Morning." He wore the same silly grin she'd observed on her own face.

"It's a mess, but we'll get it cleared."

She nodded. "What can I do?"

"You can start dragging some of the smaller limbs to the curb."

"Sure."

The chainsaw roared to life again, and he turned his attention back to the task at hand while she began clearing away what she could.

They worked in the still, humid air, the sound of chainsaws echoing around them. Sam surveyed the results of Mother Nature's temper tantrum up and down her street and wondered when power would be restored.

A half-hour later, Ethan had tackled the tree limb and stacked the wood along the curb next to her pile. He'd stacked some of the smaller pieces in the garage for use in her fireplace for the winter.

"I'm going to walk the neighborhood, see if anyone else needs help."

And her heart gave a little squeeze.

"You have anything else in the fridge that needs to be eaten before it spoils? If so, I could use something to eat."

She tilted her head and raised her hand to her forehead as the sun came out. "I think I can scare up something."

"Be back in a little while." He flashed her a grin then walked off up the street, carrying the chainsaw like a modern-day knight in shining armor. And that's when it happened. For the first time in her life, her heart—not her head—sat up and took notice.

ETHAN STROLLED BACK down the street toward Sam's, his arms and back aching, his shirt covered with wood chips and saw dust. He'd seen the power company crew earlier, so power should be restored within a couple of hours. He knew one thing: he needed a shower. And some lunch. And not necessarily in that order.

The sun had come out, heating up the atmosphere, creating an outdoor sauna. So much for the cooler weather.

Wiping sweat from his forehead with his hands, he swiped it on his pants. He looked at his T-shirt and grimaced. Filthy hand prints, some tree sap, and was that a smashed bug?

"Ethan? I thought that was you!"

He glanced over to his left, across the street from Sam's, and saw Dr. Snyder's wife. The town's biggest gossip. "Mrs. Snyder." He nodded.

"What brings you to Georgetown Square?"

"Just helping out."

"Well, aren't you handy? Is that your car parked at Samantha Love's place? I saw it there last night."

Great. "Yes." He'd just leave it at that. "Everything okay at your place? You and Joel need any help?"

"No, no. We're good. Just waiting for the electricity to come back on."

"Glad to hear all's well." Hoping she'd go back in the house, he stopped to tie his shoe, but no such luck. The old bat would stand there and watch to see if he went to Sam's.

Wondering how long it would be before the story made the gossip train, he popped his trunk, laid the chainsaw in it, and headed up the walk to Sam's door.

Sam opened the door to see where Ethan was and almost jumped out of her skin when she saw him standing on her front stoop. "Everything okay?"

"Yep."

"Lunch is ready, and I made some lemonade."

"I can't come in like this. Do you have a hose?"

"Around back. I'll bring lunch out to the screened porch."

He nodded and walked around the side of the house.

A few minutes later, she heard the screen door slam and glanced out the French doors. Fumbling with the pitcher of lemonade, she stopped in her tracks.

Ethan stood, wet T-shirt clinging to him, his hair dripping down his neck. *Holy*—That was as far as that thought got before the circuits in her brain short circuited.

"Hey, Sam! Can you bring a towel?" Ethan hollered from the porch.

Towel. Yeah. I can do that. Towels would be in the linen closet. Which is at the top of the stairs. *But you actually have to stop staring in order to go get them. Right.*

She came back through the kitchen and skidded to a halt again.

This time, he'd stripped off his shirt.

His muscular chest tapered to a hard flat stomach, and his damp jeans hung startlingly low on his hips, revealing the navy waistband of his underwear. Things it had been too dark to see the night before. But she'd let her fingers do the walking. Body Braille. Now, in the full light of day, she could see just how beautifully he was made.

He opened the door, spurring her into action.

"One towel."

"Thanks." He reached out for it, and his jeans slipped a little lower. Any lower and she'd probably faint. "I didn't want to track debris on your porch. Plus, I was damned hot."

Oh, you're hot all right, and no amount of cold water will change that. For either one of us.

As he scrubbed the towel over the hard planes of his

chest, she wondered if she should check her mouth for drool. Giving herself a mental snap-out-of-it slap, à la *Moonstruck,* she pondered those nascent feelings of lust.

The ceiling fan spun to life.

"The power! Thank goodness." Lifting her overheated face—for more reasons than the outdoor temperature—to the cooling breeze of the fan, she admonished herself for her fanciful thoughts.

Opening her eyes, her gaze found his, a sly smile on his lips. *Busted.*

Why not go for it? Lifting a brow in invitation, she asked, "Can I interest you in a shower?"

The corner of his mouth lifted. "I thought you'd never ask."

9

___

The following Wednesday, as Ethan strode down the hall for his meeting with Dr. Cosgrove, the dean of the college, he straightened his tie and tugged his shirt cuffs down.

He had an idea why Dr. Cosgrove had called the meeting.

After ushering him in to the dean's office, the receptionist asked if he'd like something to drink.

"Water. Thanks, Stacy."

"Ah, Ethan." Dr. Cosgrove entered on the heels of his assistant's departure. "Good to see you." He held out his hand to shake Ethan's. A tall, imposing man, Dr. Cosgrove had a head full of white hair, a ruddy complexion, and a ready smile. He'd been the college's dean through two presidents. Quite an accomplishment, considering the political jockeying that occurs when a member of university administration turns over.

Stacy returned with a bottle of water then quietly closed the door behind her. Dr. Cosgrove took a seat in the cozy leather chair adjacent to the sofa across from his desk.

"I understand congratulations are in order in the hiring of Dr. Danica Harding. Good job."

"Thank you." Ethan took pride in a job well-done, and he knew Dr. Harding's position with Sterling University was a feather in the department's cap, as well as in the college's.

Dr. Cosgrove clapped his hands together. "But that's not why I called this meeting."

Ethan raised a brow.

"I wanted you to be the first in the college to know that I'm retiring. Candice and I are ready to spend more time with the grandkids."

He hadn't seen that coming. "Congratulations. You've earned it."

"That I have. And I think you're in the market for a deanship."

Oh. Well. "I guess I've been pretty transparent."

"That, and I've always known you were dean material. Sterling would be crazy to let you slip out the door. So I'm recommending you as interim dean, and I strongly suggest that you put in for the position when it's posted."

Stunned, Ethan didn't know what to say. "Thank you. I'm, well . . . I'm speechless."

"A professor who's speechless. That's a first."

If Ethan were to get the job, it would create a problem with Sam. Sterling had a nepotism policy, and as dean of the college, her department would report to him. It would also create a problem with his mother's job, which he'd talked her into, and which she'd come to love.

"If you don't mind, I'd like to give it some thought."

"Of course. Would a week give you enough time?"

"Yes."

∼

"Dr. Love! Sam!" At the sound of his voice, Sam picked up her pace heading for her car. Ethan!

When he'd left the afternoon after the storm—and her first experience with shower sex—there had been no promises. No plans. And she was okay with that. She wasn't looking for a relationship. It was just sex, right?

She'd never had a purely sexual relationship because, well, given her sexual hang-ups, she hadn't really seen the point. Now, she didn't know how to behave. What was expected of her. And what she should expect. *Like, oh, I don't know . . . communication?*

No phone calls, no text messages, nothing. Not even a smoke signal. And she hated that the lack of communication bothered her.

She opened her car door, tossed her bag in the front seat then faced him, her hand on the top of the door, her blood boiling. "What?"

"Hi."

Damn! Why did he have to smile like that. Why did he have to look at her with those warm brown eyes? *Do not say it!* "Why haven't you called?" *Dammit. You had to say it, didn't you?*

"I'm sorry. I've been in negotiations with a prospective faculty member. You remember, I told you? The one who would bring with her a Nobel Prize in literature?"

Yep. He'd told her. She'd just forgotten. Her anger dissipated. But then he hadn't told her he would be *incommunicado*. Her anger returned. She leveled him with a glare.

"What? Are you mad?" He chuckled, which only raised her ire. Then he stepped into her, invading the space between the car door and the passenger compartment. His hands went to her shoulders, as he gazed into her eyes.

She glanced around, uncomfortable with his close proximity in public. She didn't want to start any tongues wagging. Unless it was theirs. In each other's mouths.

"I'm sorry. I should have called. Forgive me?"

Geez. Just one touch from him and she was ready to melt into a simpering puddle of womanhood. She nodded.

"Good. Listen, it's my mom's birthday on Friday, and I'm having dinner with her. I'd like you to come with me if you're free."

Dinner with his mom? She didn't know what to make of that. Apparently wariness was written all over her face because he cajoled, "Come on. You'd make us both very happy."

"Um, sure. What time?"

"I'll pick you up at six."

She nodded.

"I've got to run. Department meeting. I'll call you later." He tried to kiss her on the mouth, but she turned her cheek. They'd already put on quite the spectacle in the faculty parking lot. And she didn't do spectacle.

"So, let me get this straight. It's your mom's birthday, but she's cooking?" Sam asked from the passenger seat.

"That's correct."

Sam shook her head and Ethan chuckled. Flipping on his blinker, he turned into his childhood neighborhood. This is just what he needed—a distraction from the pros and cons of the job as interim dean colliding in his head. "She loves to cook. And when it comes to cooking for those she loves, she couldn't think of anything better."

Driving down the street, he passed Nash's childhood

home, where his father still lived. Then Suzy Stringfellow's house on the right. Her parents finally put it on the market—planning to retire to Florida. Young couples were invading the modest neighborhood looking for affordable first homes. His mom and Nash's father were the last holdouts.

Pulling into the driveway, he threw the car into park. "This is it."

Sam took in the manicured front yard with its beds of colorful petunias, the trimmed boxwoods lining the sidewalk to the front door, and the porch with its hanging baskets of Boston ferns. "You grew up here?"

He nodded. "Me and my sister."

"I like it." She opened the car door and stood a moment, looking around the neighborhood.

"It's small, but it's home." Ethan came around the car and took her hand. "There's Mom now."

His mom stood on the front porch, dishtowel over her shoulder, a smile on her face. Hard to believe today was her sixtieth birthday. Patting the little box in his jacket pocket, he guided Sam up the walk.

"Hi, Mrs. Quinn," Sam greeted her.

"Margaret, remember?"

"Of course."

"Don't you look a picture?" his mom said, as she took Sam's hand and kissed her cheek.

And his mom was right. Sam did look a picture. Her red hair back in a ponytail, an emerald-green sundress flirting with her matching eyes, and sexy little sandals with those Jezebel-red toenails.

"Come on in. I hope you're hungry. We've got pot roast, green beans, roasted potatoes, and homemade apple pie for dessert."

After eating what amounted to enough food for a week, Sam took Margaret's refusal of help in the kitchen as an opportunity to peruse the photos displayed about the tidy living room.

The red-brick fireplace mantel held photos of Ethan as a boy, alongside photos of a girl who must be his sister. Ethan in a football uniform, kneeling, his helmet under his arm, another of him, a baseball bat on his shoulder and a cap pulled down low over his eyes. Finally, one of him in a cap and gown, apparently his high-school graduation picture. He wore the wry grin she'd come to recognize. The one that said, *Yeah, I'm just as surprised as you.*

On the bookshelf next to the fireplace stood photos of his parents—wedding-day photos, picnics, birthdays. Their mutual respect for one another clear in every snapshot. How she would have loved to have had them in her study.

Margaret and Ethan had shared stories over dinner about family vacations, nothing extravagant, just fishing and camping trips, s'mores by the campfire, swimming in the lake. Simple, meaningful experiences.

Her parents didn't take vacations. They took sabbaticals and were usually holed-up in some Italian villa or French chateau working on their latest bestseller. She had no photo albums filled with memories. No one with whom to reminisce. Shaking off her maudlin thoughts, she returned to her exploration.

Below the photos, the shelves were stuffed with books. The very ones Ethan said he and his father had read together.

Hands rested on her waist, and Ethan leaned in to kiss her shoulder then rested his chin there.

"You have an amazing family." She settled back against him as if it was the most natural thing in the world.

"Yeah, I do. Even my sister, Charlotte, has her moments." He turned Sam to face him, "What about you? Any brothers or sisters?"

She shook her head. "No. Just me."

"Cousins?"

"No." Being an only child had never bothered her, but for some reason her answer left behind an unfamiliar ache.

"Well, you can share mine." He pointed to a group in a photo—kids and adults, young and old. "The Quinn family reunion the summer before my grandmother died. Thirty-two of us in all."

"Wow. How do you remember all their names?"

"I'm not sure I do. Mom," he called into the kitchen, "who's the guy in the John Deere cap with the pipe in his mouth?"

"That's your late Uncle Arty. You know, Aunt Zelda's husband?"

"Oh, yeah."

"Dessert," his mom called back.

"None of my clothes are going to fit after this meal," Sam said, as she ran her hands down her stomach.

"Then I guess you'll just have to go naked. Such a pity."

SAM WAS quiet on the drive back into Sterling, but it was a companionable silence. Ethan liked that they could just be in each other's company and not feel the need to fill it with chatter. He reached over, took her hand, and received a soft smile in return.

He'd been giving it a lot of thought. Work complications

notwithstanding, he'd like to take this relationship to the next level—exclusivity. Not that he'd been seeing anyone else. And as far as he knew, neither had she. But he'd like to make it official.

Not only was Sam beautiful, she was smart and funny. And while she said she didn't believe in romance, her actions spoke differently.

He'd seen the wistful expression on her face when his mom spoke of his dad. He'd observed the tender touch of her fingertip as she'd skimmed it along his parents' wedding photo. The way she'd reacted to the bouquet he'd brought to her. She'd been surprised and touched.

Maybe she said she didn't believe in romance because she'd never *experienced* it. He just needed to show her; then she'd believe.

And while she might declare otherwise, even to herself, she yearned to belong. To a family. To someone who would cherish her. Someone with whom she could make memories.

While he'd stood at the sink drying dishes after dinner, his mom had told him how much she liked Sam, not so subtly hinting that she was daughter-in-law material.

He wasn't ready to walk down the aisle yet, but a relationship? Yeah, he could do that. And who knew? Maybe one day they would take that walk down the aisle. Make those memories she so clearly craved.

But first, he'd set the mood with some romance of his own, then he'd tell her how he felt about her.

As Sam walked up the sidewalk to her front door, her hand clasped with Ethan's, she thought again of the pretty little necklace he had given his mom for her birthday. A custom arrangement of birthstones—hers, his, his sister's, and his late father's. Such a thoughtful gift. His mother had cried as he placed it around her neck. Happy tears, she'd said.

There was no arguing that, with him, it was the little things that counted.

She hadn't exactly been engaging on the ride home, but only because she'd been deep in thought, and oddly, a little envious of Ethan's childhood.

By all accounts, he'd grown up in a warm, loving home, maintained long-term friendships with the kids in his neighborhood, like his best friend, Nash Taylor. He'd lived in the same town, the same house, until he was eighteen years old. Whereas, she'd pulled up stakes every two or three years at the whim of her parents' careers.

Delaney was the closest thing she'd ever had to a best friend, and they'd known each other less than a year. Ethan and Nash had known each other since grade school.

What would it be like to have someone know you inside and out, and like you despite your shortcomings?

What nonsense. Must've been the walk down memory lane that Ethan and his mother had taken over dinner that left her feeling bereft. If she wanted to reach the pinnacle of her career, she'd be pulling up stakes in another year or two to move onward and upward.

"Would you like to come in?" Sam asked, as she unlocked her door.

"Sure."

She'd barely closed the door behind them when he'd snagged her around the waist and covered her mouth with his. Dropping her purse where she stood, she raised her arms, wrapping them around his neck. Ethan Quinn had turned her into a nymphomaniac. She'd been thinking about getting him back in her bed all evening.

"God, I've been dying to do that since I picked you up three hours ago," he murmured against her lips.

Walking her backward into the living room, they fell back on the couch, his long, lean body covering hers. Relishing the weight of him on her, she tugged his mouth down to hers. Tongues circling, breaths mingling. Such poignant sweetness.

He sat up, gazed down at her, his hair mussed from her frantic fingers. Lifting her head, he freed her hair from its tie, spreading it across her shoulders. "So beautiful."

Reaching up, she began flicking open the buttons on his dress shirt, tugging it free from his waistband. She spread her hands along his rib cage. "You're not too bad yourself, Dr. Quinn."

He sucked in a breath as her fingers grazed his stomach, heading south. "Take me to bed, Ethan."

"Your wish is my command." Scooping her up, he threw her over his shoulder in a fireman's carry.

She barked out a laugh at his unexpected action. As he climbed the stairs, he smacked her ass. She yelped, then dissolved into a fit of giggles.

Sex had never been so much fun.

"You think that's funny, huh?"

"Yes," she choked out.

He dropped her onto the bed and tossed the skirt of her dress up, covering her face. Her giggles died the moment he shoved her panties aside and covered her with his mouth.

～

STRETCHED OUT NEXT TO ETHAN, his warm hard body against hers, she sighed in contentment and thought about what she'd been missing all of her adult life—incredible, breathtaking, mind-blowing sex.

Ethan rose, propping himself up with his elbow, and gazed down at her. He brushed his fingertips along her cheekbones. "You know, I can't help the rush of male pride in the post-sex flush in your cheeks."

She rolled her eyes but blushed all the same.

Settling his hand on her stomach, he continued. "So, I received some interesting news the other day, but it's not for public consumption."

"Didn't anyone ever tell you that pillow-talk is confidential?" She reached up and ran her fingers through his hair.

"Now that you mention it . . ." he replied with a grin. "Dr. Cosgrove is retiring."

"Oh. That's nice."

"And he's not only recommending they appoint me interim dean, but also that I apply for the permanent position."

"That's incredible, Ethan. Congratulations." She couldn't help the smile that stretched across her face.

"Too soon for congratulations. It's not a done deal yet."

Then she recalled the conversation they'd had in Ruby's Diner the day her car battery died, about why they shouldn't date: the university's nepotism policy. His argument had been that neither one reported to the other. That wouldn't be the case anymore.

Now, when she'd put aside her reasons for avoiding any kind of relationship with him. Now, when she'd begun to crave his company. So would he be the one to end this? Or should she end it before she descended any deeper into this . . . whatever it was?

"I see the wheels turning in that pretty head of yours," he said, as she sat up and shoved her hair out of her face.

"That means—"

He cradled her face in his warm hand. "I know. But I'm working on it. There has to be a solution."

"And what if there's not? What if—"

"You think too much." He touched his lips to hers, as his hand skimmed down her neck and along her shoulder.

"But—"

He pressed a finger to her lips, effectively shushing her. Anger surged through her as she prepared to tell him exactly what she thought about being stifled. Then his lips replaced his finger and his hand cupped the back of her head, easing back down on the mattress. Her head said "resist," but her heart and body said "surrender." Sighing, she raised the white flag.

10

———

"So, you and that pretty new professor, Dr. Love . . . ?"

"How'd you know?" Ethan huffed out as he and Nash took an early-morning run.

Nash lifted a sweaty brow. "Did you forget where you live?"

Right. The gossip train of Sterling was a well-oiled machine. He should have known it was only a matter of time, especially after Mrs. Snyder caught him. He let that go, as the sound of their feet struck the pavement. "Who told you?"

"Colleen Dukakis told Ginny Decker, who told Grady Morgan, who told me."

Great. Even Nash's coaching staff got in on the fun.

"When were you planning to tell me?" Nash lifted the hem of his ratty Denver Broncos T-shirt and wiped his face.

"Sorry, *Dad*, I didn't know I needed your permission to date someone."

Nash snorted. "Not just someone. Samantha Love, daughter of the famous 'Love Doctors.' And subject of the dating pool your assistant won."

God, would he ever live that down? "And your point is?"

"My point is, apparently this has been going on a few weeks. Is it serious?"

Was it serious? For him it was. He wasn't sure about Sam. She played her cards close to her vest. "Maybe." It was the best he could do.

"Just watch yourself. Don't get hooked on this woman if she doesn't plan to set down roots. I know you like a brother. You'll never leave this area. I just hate to see you get hurt again."

By hurt, Nash meant Julie. If she'd stayed, they would have been married a year now. She might've even been pregnant. But then again, no. She didn't want the interruption to her career. "I'm good." He felt Nash's eyes on his face. "Really."

They ran in silence a few paces, just the sound of their feet against the pavement and their labored breathing, in tune with one another as if blood brothers.

"There is something I want to talk to you about, though," Ethan said.

"Sounds serious."

"This is confidential."

"Goes without saying."

"The dean of my college is retiring. He's recommending they name me interim. He's also recommending I apply for the permanent position."

"Man, that's the best news I've heard all day!" Nash slapped him on the shoulder. "It's what you've wanted for so long."

"Yeah, but there's a problem." He took a swig from his water bottle, wiped his mouth.

"Your mom."

"And Sam."

"Look, Ethan. It sounds like you and Sam are pretty seri-ous, but you haven't put a ring on her finger yet, so don't put your career on hold. You owe it to yourself to explore this. Take the interim position. Who knows? It might really suck," he said with a grin. "Problem solved."

STROLLING OVER TO UNCOMMON GROUNDS, the campus coffee shop, later that day, Ethan pulled together the perfect plan to raise the subject of a serious relationship with Sam.

He'd ask her if she'd like to go to the annual Founder's Day Parade and Fair two weeks from Saturday and then catch dinner and a movie in Carlyle afterward. A lot of handholding, a little ice-cream sharing, very subtle romance. Then when the moment was right, he'd bring up the idea of an exclusive arrangement.

What he didn't have a plan for was what to do about their relationship while he was interim. Or, what's more, if he went after it and got the permanent position.

Well, at this point he didn't know if she would say yes. He'd cross that bridge when he came to it.

The little bell jingled when he opened the door and stepped inside the welcoming cool of the AC. Spotting the subject of his musings standing in line, he couldn't stop the grin that spread across his face.

She juggled a tote bag, a handbag, and a smartphone. Her fiery red hair was in an intricate braid, and the silky white blouse and navy pencil skirt hugged her subtle curves. Sensible flats graced her feet.

He stepped up behind her and whispered in her ear, "Just who I was looking for."

She gasped and turned toward his mouth, and he

quickly leaned in to take advantage, pressing a kiss to those lovely lips. She swayed toward him for the briefest moment, before remembering their public surroundings.

"You were looking for me?"

"Yeah. That, and a little iced caffeine."

She shrugged her tote bag back up on her shoulder.

"Give me that." He slipped his hand beneath the strap and slid it down her arm then threw it over his shoulder. "Why women carry tote bags and handbags the size of small cars is a mystery to me."

"We have a lot of stuff, and I was coming from my last class."

Next in line, she gave the barista her order then tucked her smartphone into the voluminous bag that served as a purse.

Before the barista could ring up Sam's order, Ethan ordered an iced coffee. "I've got hers as well." Taking a twenty out of his wallet, he handed it to the tattoo-decorated girl.

"You didn't have to buy my coffee."

"I know I didn't."

"But thanks."

After receiving their orders, they proceeded out the door. "Where are you headed?" Ethan asked.

"Back to my office."

"Perfect. I'll walk with you."

A sidewalk wound its way through a particularly lovely section of campus, where moss-covered oaks offered a welcome respite from the hot sun. In spring, the azaleas and dogwoods wore showy flowers, and in fall, the Japanese maples sported leaves in shades of red and purple.

Students sat at picnic tables scattered beneath the trees. Others sat on the ground, computers in their laps, while still others used their backpacks as pillows and stretched out for afternoon naps.

Ethan loved the energy of the campus. The debates, the intellectual discourse. And, spying a couple nuzzling one another behind a giant live oak, the romance.

He glanced over at Sam. "What are you doing on August twenty-fifth?"

A frown creased her brow. "Why? What's August twenty-fifth?"

"It's Sterling's Founder's Day. There's a parade followed by a fair with food and craft vendors. It's a pretty big deal."

"A big deal, huh?" She smiled at him, and his heart stuttered in his chest. He'd never grow tired of that smile. The way her green eyes sparkled. The dimples he wanted to kiss. "Well, then I guess I'd better go."

"Yeah. You don't want to be labeled a pariah by the locals for failing to pay tribute to our benefactors."

"No. I wouldn't want that." She tucked an errant lock of hair behind her ear. "But who would I go with?" she asked with a wry grin.

"Hmm. That's a good question." He tapped his chin with his finger. "I suppose I could take you. You know, to save you from the scorn."

She nodded, her expression serious. "A selfless deed then?"

He shrugged. "I'm nothing if not selfless."

"Then I accept. After all, I wouldn't want your noble sacrifice to go unappreciated."

"Thank you." He gave her a shoulder bump. "And if I'm not mistaken, Dr. Love, you're flirting with me."

"I don't flirt."

"If you say so."

Giving instructions to her new graduate assistant, Lisa Reynolds, Sam handed her a stack of student papers. "I'll need the grades entered by tomorrow, noon."

"No problem," Lisa said, then gathered her backpack. "Anything else?"

"Not at the moment."

"See you tomorrow then."

What a relief to finally have a new assistant. Now maybe she could get caught up.

Her phone buzzed with an incoming text.

Good morning, Dr. Love. I hope you slept well.

Sam snorted. He knew very well how she'd slept.

I got very little sleep.

Momentarily, her phone buzzed again.

Complaining?

She smiled as she thumbed her response.

No, but I nearly fell asleep during my own lecture.

Seconds later.

It's not my fault your topic is boring.

"Humph."

You must be confusing my lecture with yours.

His reply arrived shortly.

Ouch! How about lunch later? You can pull the knife from my heart.

Smiling, she contemplated her reply. She'd like to go, but . . .

Can't. I'm meeting with a student. See a doctor about that knife wound.

She waited, wondering if she'd really hurt his feelings. Her phone buzzed.

There's nothing to cure what ails me. I'll call you later. XOXO

She stared at her phone, a no-doubt goofy smile on her face.

Okay, enough of that. She had a backlog of blood samples to run through her assay. Setting aside her phone, she rounded her desk and headed for her lab. Word had spread, and every unattached female, and a few attached ones, were flocking to her lab to sign up for her study. Most were disappointed to learn they wouldn't get the results until the study was closed, and only if their match had also agreed.

But given the recent influx, she'd reached her enrollment goal for females, and she only needed a few more men. Then, she could close the study, and run the final data analysis. With Sterling's access to a super-computing facility in Atlanta, the number-crunching wouldn't take long. The program had already been written and tested.

When she got to her lab, she noticed that the results from her latest batch had popped up on her computer screen. Pulling the code key, she began running the data to match it to the questionnaires. Of the twenty new blood tests she'd run against the existing database, two were matches.

And she recognized one of the identifiers: Subject 7645. Ethan Quinn.

"Are the rumors true?" Melinda asked Ethan as soon as he walked into the office from his meeting with the dean. The provost agreed to the interim dean appointment and

strongly encouraged Ethan to put his name in for the permanent position.

He frowned, thinking she was talking about him and Sam. "What rumors?"

Handing him his mail, she leaned forward and whispered, "Dr. Cosgrove is retiring and you're going to be dean."

No matter how hard you tried, there was no such thing as secrets in academia.

"I don't know what you're talking about," Ethan lied, as he shuffled through his stack of mail.

"So, it *is* true."

At his lifted brow, she smirked. "You don't lie very well."

Melinda had been with him too long. "Come into my office."

She rose with alacrity and followed him into his office, shutting the door behind her.

He tossed his mail onto his desk then perched a hip against it. "Dr. Cosgrove is retiring. I have been asked to take over as interim until the search for a new dean is completed."

She rubbed her hands together in delight. "And you're applying, right?"

Ethan sighed. The woman was irrepressible. "Yes."

"Yes!" she said, with a fist-pump.

"Now, don't get the cart before the horse. I'm not a shoe-in."

"I beg to differ. I'd be willing to bet—"

He groaned. "Don't tell me there's another pool."

"No. Not yet, anyway," she said with a grin.

"Look, I'd appreciate it if you'd keep this between us."

"You know me better than that." She drew herself up, clearly affronted. "I may like to listen to the gossip, but I don't participate."

Sighing, he rubbed his face. "I know."

She turned and headed for the door, but stopped short, her hand on the knob. "What happens to your relationship with Dr. Love if you become dean?"

Good question. Too bad he didn't have an answer.

STILL REELING from her latest results, Sam headed out her front door for a much-needed run. She craved the distraction, not to mention the endorphins. Escaping campus as soon as her meeting was over, she'd avoided bumping into Ethan.

Ethan was the first person in her database to have a duplicate match. Of course, it was bound to happen. People are compatible with more than one person, right? A widower finds companionship again after his first wife dies. It's a wonder this is the first double-match.

But why Ethan? And Jackie Ledbetter, of all people! And why did she care? She didn't even want to be his match. She didn't want *any* match. Right? Right.

Picking up her pace, she ran up a hill toward a nature path she'd discovered last week. The peace and solitude of the woods would do her good.

"Jesus!" A squirrel darted in front of her, startling her.

This whole thing with Ethan had been ridiculous from the start. Him and his romance. Well, he could romance Jackie Ledbetter. She seemed willing enough.

She'd let the ever-charming Ethan Quinn get into her head, not to mention her bed. He'd helped her discover her passionate side, but he'd also become a colossal distraction. And one she could ill-afford right now.

It was time to put the brakes on and refocus her energies

on her work. Her career, her professional reputation, were more important than a fling with a sexy colleague.

LATER THAT AFTERNOON, relaxed after her run and confident in her decision, Sam stood in line at the Piggly Wiggly, unloading her shopping basket when she heard her name.

"And he spent the whole night at her house the night of that big storm."

"Oh. No. He. Didn't!"

"Oh. Yes. He. Did! Marjorie Snyder saw him cutting up downed limbs the next morning. *After* seeing his car there all night."

One line over, two clerical assistants from her college gossiped over their grocery carts.

"I bet thunder wasn't the only thing rattling the house."

"And you know who her parents are?"

The other girl snickered. "The *Love* Doctors."

"No wonder he's sniffing around her. She probably knows her way around in the bedroom."

More giggling.

Sam felt sick. So much for the endorphins. Cortisol flooded her system as they continued their gossip.

"Well, I saw them in the faculty parking lot the other day, and the body language—let me tell you, she is all into him."

"And I heard he'd invited her to his momma's house."

"And you know what that means . . . no Southern gentleman brings a girl home to momma unless it's serious."

"Uh-huh. You got that right."

"'Course, what did you expect, after Melinda Wilson won that pool?"

A pool? What kind of pool? A swimming pool? What did that have to do with her and Ethan?

"She figured he'd be the first to take her out. After years as his assistant, seems to me that's what you'd call a sure thing."

"She won a boatload of money, too!"

A betting pool? There'd been a betting *pool over* her? Her blood began to boil. Was he in on the pool? Was this all just a game to him?

One of the women giggled. "I wonder if there was a bet on how long before he slept with her."

What the—

"Didn't take long," the other woman responded.

Sam gasped.

"Ma'am? Ma'am?"

Sam realized the clerk was talking to her. "I'm sorry?"

"That'll be $45.56."

"Right."

Ethan Quinn, you're dead meat.

11

———

"I really need to get a housekeeper," Ethan muttered to himself as he ran the vacuum over the carpet. He'd sent Sam a text earlier asking her to dinner at his place, and although she hadn't texted back yet, he got a jump on making his home presentable. He'd paid special attention to his bedroom and bath. Clean sheets and towels, a candle on the side of the big soaker tub he never used. Maybe that would change tonight.

He'd run out to the store later for a couple of steaks, a nice bottle of Merlot, maybe run by Connie's Confectionaire for dessert.

He'd been spending a lot of time at Sam's place, but he wanted her in his home, in his bed. Maybe the caveman in him wanted to show her he could provide the basic human needs: food, shelter, and romance.

Putting away the vacuum, he couldn't recall having been happier.

Sam could be prickly, sure. Especially when she retreated behind that reserved professional guise. But he'd seen her open and warm, laughing, those green eyes sparkling like emeralds. He'd also seen her scared and vulnerable, like the night of the storm. No, Sam may come off as aloof to people who didn't know her, but the woman behind the façade was anything but.

SAM KNOCKED on Ethan's front door, steam escaping from her ears.

The door flew open. "Sam! You're a little early for dinner." A smile lit his face, but it quickly turned to a frown when he read her facial expression.

"I need to talk to you."

Ethan had on workout shorts that hung low on his hips and a holey T-shirt that read LIT HAPPENS. Dammit, why did he have to look sexy no matter what he wore? *Focus.*

"Sounds serious. Come in."

Although this was the first time in his house, she put her curiosity on hold as she tore into him. "Was this all just a game to you?"

"What are you talking about?"

"Do you go around romancing every new female professor on campus, betting you'll be the first to go out with her. To *sleep* with her?"

"Whoa." He raised his hands. "Wait a minute. Are you talking about the pool?"

"Damn right, I am." She poked him in his chest. *Ow.* His very hard chest. "How could you? How could you make me think you were Mr. Romance, when really, all you are is Mr. Get-In-My-Pants? How dare you?"

"Sam, I wasn't involved in that pool. I didn't start it, I didn't put my name in it, and I certainly didn't put any money in it."

He took her by the shoulders and leveled her with a look. "Sam, I can't control what other people do. I don't deserve the blame for someone else's actions. I'm sorry I didn't tell you about it, though. I should have."

She pulled free and paced into his living room, her nerves humming with anger and frustration.

"Did you know we're the subject of gossip?"

From the look on his face, he did. "Sam, when you work and live in a small college town, gossip is part of the package."

She pointed in the direction of the grocery store. "I was standing in line at the Piggly Wiggly, my name being bandied about like some town slut." Tears clogged her throat. She would not cry. "My personal and professional reputations are of utmost importance to me. Professionally, I've had to work hard to separate myself, and my work, from that of my parents. And given my chosen field, I often have to defend myself to skeptics who don't take my science seriously."

"Sam—"

She held up her index finger. "I'm not done. Personally, because first boys, and then *grown* men, assumed I was loose, I've strived to maintain an impeccable reputation, seeking to avoid adding fuel to the fire. Even with my carefully protected reputation, I still deal with the snide remarks about my parents' work and my own sexuality."

Ethan stepped into her, settling his hands at her waist, making it difficult for her to continue her tirade. "Sam, people only gossip when you're behaving as if you've got something to hide. So, let's come out of the closet. Take our relationship public. That will stop the gossip mill."

"I don't want a relationship with you." She threw her hands up in the air. "What else do you want me to say? I don't really see the point anyway, Ethan. If you become dean, we *can't* have a relationship . . . unless I leave, and while Sterling is just a stopover in my career, I'm not willing to sacrifice my career for the sake of yours."

Ethan rubbed his chest, where it felt as if he'd been kicked by a horse. Taking a mental step back, he searched her face, and what he saw there was fear. Putting his hurt aside, he approached her again. "Sam, where is this coming from? Why do you keep retreating behind this wall of fear?"

"Where is what coming from? I've been trying to tell you all along that I didn't want this, but you were bound and determined to prove me wrong."

"I wasn't trying to prove anything."

"Weren't you?" She narrowed her eyes, which currently spit green sparks. "You saw me, and my science, as a challenge. Not something to be respected, but something to be refuted. I can't be with someone who doesn't respect me, or my work."

Okay, that was a low blow. He held up his index finger to make his point. "I never once said I didn't respect you or your work. I may not agree with your theories, but disagreement doesn't equate to disrespect."

She folded her arms across her chest and turned her back to him.

Closing the mile-wide gap between them, he placed his hands on her shoulders. "Sam, tell me what's holding you back. Tell me what you're so afraid of."

Shrugging off his hands, she said, "Nothing. I'm not afraid of anything. I don't want a relationship with you, or with anyone, for that matter. Why can't you understand that?" She stalked over to his door, yanking it open. "I'm asking you to please just leave me alone."

Walking through the front door, and out of his life, Sam closed the barrier between them with a final soft click.

Ethan stood in the middle of his living room wondering what the hell had just happened. He'd gone from happiness to despair in the time it took to boil an egg.

He released a mirthless laugh. "Well, guess that solved the nepotism issue."

TWO WEEKS after Sam broke up with him, Ethan dropped into his desk chair and scrubbed a hand over his face. He should be elated. He'd at least attained an interim dean position. But instead, he just felt empty. Not only did he not have someone to share in his accomplishment, the accomplishment itself had lost its appeal.

He'd done it again. Placed his heart in the hands of a woman who had no intention of staying in Sterling. No intention of putting down roots.

He'd seen Sam from across the parking lot that morning, gathering her things from the backseat of her POS car before heading into the building. She'd never once looked in his direction. Either she didn't see him, or she was ignoring him.

Melanie entered, a stack of messages in her hand. "Congratulations, Dean Quinn—"

"Interim," he corrected.

She shrugged. "That's only temporary." She frowned. "What's wrong? I thought you'd be . . . I don't know, happier?"

"Nothing. Just a lot on my mind."

"Like Dr. Love?"

He held back a retort. "No. That's . . . over. And I sure as hell hope there was no pool for that."

Melanie crossed her arms over her chest, her mouth a thin line. "Should I arrange for the movers?"

"No. I'll stay put until the search for a permanent dean is concluded."

"But—"

"No. I don't want to move twice if I don't have to." And now he wasn't even sure he wanted the job.

"Suit yourself then." She turned to leave then stopped before she reached the door. "I'm sorry about Sam."

No sorrier than he.

SAM HAD FINALLY RECEIVED some good news: The patent application had been granted. Now the university could finalize the license deal with SoulMates.com.

The final study data was remarkable actually. She'd received a voice message from the company CEO to give him a call. Probably just wanted to talk about the deal, maybe offer some words of congratulation.

She'd moped around long enough. It was time to get her head back in the game and focus not only on the TED Talk she'd been asked to give but on her latest theory. Clearly, Ethan's double-match indicated her test was not infallible, but she had some ideas for refining the testing.

Taking a deep, calming breath, she picked up the phone on her desk and dialed Perry Childers, SoulMates.com's CEO.

"This is Perry."

She was momentarily dumbstruck. She'd expected an assistant, not the man himself.

"Hello?"

"Oh, Mr. Childers, this is Dr. Love. I'm returning your call."

"Dr. Love. What a fortuitous name. Thank you for calling me back. I'll get straight to it. I love your assay—no pun intended—I'm impressed with the results of your study, and I'd like to make you my VP of Research."

If she could see her expression right now, she knew it would be one of shock and awe.

"Dr. Love? You there?"

"Um, yes. Yes, I'm here. Sorry, I . . . Well, I wasn't expecting that." She pressed her hand to her stomach, hoping to calm the riot of butterflies there.

"I'd love to fly you out. First class, of course. Take you on a tour of our campus, show you what we have to offer. What do you say?"

She scrubbed at the lines she knew were forming on her forehead. What did she have to lose? "I . . . Sure. That would be wonderful."

"Great. I'll have my assistant, Isabel, contact you with a detailed itinerary."

"Thank you, Mr. Childers."

"I look forward to meeting you. And, please, call me Perry."

GRABBING a to-go lunch from Ruby's, Ethan saw Delaney at a booth with some other professors from her department. Approaching the table, he nodded to everyone.

"Hi, Ethan." Delaney offered him a sad smile. *Great. Just what he needed—sympathy from the jilter's best friend.*

"Can I talk to you a minute?"

"Um, sure." Delaney rose from the table and followed him over to a quieter corner of the diner.

"Have you seen Sam? I've been looking all over for her, and she's not answering my phone calls or text messages." He really needed to meet with her. He didn't want any awkwardness between them now that he was interim dean. It was important that their previous relationship not affect the morale of the college.

Delaney gnawed on her lower lip, a look of uncertainty on her face. "She didn't tell you?"

His gut clinched. "Tell me what?"

"Sam is in San Francisco meeting with the online-dating service who licensed her assay about a job."

If she'd told him Sam was getting married, he couldn't have been more shocked. When Sam had said Sterling was just a rung on her career ladder, she wasn't kidding. But even so, he didn't expect her to leave so soon. And to leave academia for private industry.

Delaney touched his arm. "You okay?"

"I'm fine." His free hand clenched into a fist. Some time in the gym with Nash and a punching bag was in order.

Delaney's concerned gaze made him uncomfortable. "I've got to run to a meeting." He nodded then strode out of the diner, handing off his lunch to a student walking by. "Here. I've lost my appetite."

"Thanks, dude!"

Thunder rumbled overhead as he made his way through town back to campus. Just as he passed beneath the main gates, the clouds opened up. "Sure. Why not," he muttered.

WITH A GLASS of champagne at her elbow, Sam sat back in her luxurious first-class seat and sighed in satisfaction.

She hadn't expected to fall in love with a job, but that was before she'd spent an amazing two days at SoulMates.com's Silicon Valley campus, touring the facilities, which reportedly rivaled that of Google. Employee cafeteria that served only organic, locally-sourced foods. A dry cleaners, medical clinic, hair salon, state-of-the-art fitness center, and daycare right on the grounds.

Perry and his executive team had wined and dined her. They had big plans for her compatibility assay, and for her, if she liked the job. And what wasn't to like?

The research staff who would report to her were top-notch. Her office had a spectacular view of the Santa Clara Valley, and the salary and bonus package were off the charts.

A real-estate agent had shown her some properties in the Bay Area, and with the salary they were offering, she could actually afford them. She'd pay off her student loans, buy a new car . . .

It had all happened so fast.

She hadn't given Perry an answer, telling him she'd like to mull it over, but she was leaning heavily in favor of it.

She'd have to put her place up for sale. Or maybe rent it out. Delaney really liked the place. Maybe she'd take it.

Delaney. She closed her eyes. In her excitement, she didn't think about leaving her best friend. The only one she'd ever had. Delaney had been very excited but also apprehensive and disappointed at the possibility of losing her best friend so soon. But Delaney could always come out to visit, right?

And then there was Ethan.

Who was she kidding? *You broke up with him, remember?* It was the right decision, she told herself for the umpteenth time. Then why did it hurt every time she thought about him?

Even if she wanted a relationship with him, which could never work, of course, he'd never leave Sterling. And a long-distance relationship with the entire continental U.S. between them would never work. And if she stayed, there was the insurmountable nepotism issue.

With time and distance between them, she wondered why she'd said the things she did. Anger? Hurt? Or, as Ethan had said, fear?

Maybe her parents' career moves weren't the only thing to blame for her lack of close friendships. Which circled her thoughts back to Delaney. Could their friendship last, or would they drift apart, phone calls and emails growing more infrequent, until the only communication they had was birthday and Christmas cards?

Her head began to ache, along with her heart, as the initial enthusiasm turned to anxiety, and the pleasure of success turned hollow.

12

———

Ethan threw a punch at the bag Nash held, catching him unawares and knocking him off balance. Nash replanted his feet. Ethan would have preferred a good old-fashioned brawl without any protective padding–maybe the pain from a well-delivered punch would replace the pain in his chest where his heart used to be before Sam ripped it out and stomped on it. But the last thing Nash needed was to have his brains bouncing around inside his skull like a pinball.

Even so, Nash egged him on, and it didn't take much for Ethan to light into the bag. A few punches later and Nash released the bag and threw up his hands in surrender. "Damn. You trying to give me another concussion?"

Guilt washed over Ethan. "Sorry man."

"What's eating you, anyway?" Nash walked over to the bench where they'd dropped their gym bags.

Ethan followed him over and sat while Nash helped him remove his gloves. "Nothing."

"Bullshit."

Ethan picked up a bottle of Gatorade and guzzled it.

Wiping his mouth, he replaced he cap then tossed the empty bottle into the trashcan across from them.

"The last time you hit the bag like that Julie had just left you." Nash narrowed his eyes. "Shit. She didn't?"

Ethan sighed. That's what happened when you'd been friends since grade school. You could read each other's minds.

"Where's she off to?"

"San Francisco." Ethan wiped the sweat off his face and neck with a towel then opened his gym bag for some water.

"Well, hell. Nothing like moving across the country to put a damper on a relationship."

"Even if she wasn't leaving, she said she didn't want a relationship with me." Tossing back the bottle of water, he took several gulps.

"Ouch. Did she say why? Not good-looking enough? Not great in the sack?"

Ethan held up his middle finger. "Asshat."

Nash chuckled and slapped him on the shoulder. "Let's go grab a beer and you can tell me all about it."

THE SUN HAD JUST SET when Sam drove past the Sterling City Limit sign. Releasing a breath, some of the tension gripping her neck and shoulders most of the drive from the Atlanta airport dissipated at the sight of Sterling University's red brick clock tower. Passing the main entrance to campus, she thought about how beautiful the school was. Collegiate gothic buildings surrounded by ancient oaks. In spring, dogwoods, redbuds, and azaleas put on a show. And when she'd arrived last fall, the trees welcomed her with their brilliant red, orange, and yellow foliage.

Look at her waxing poetic. She shook her head. Jet lag.

She thought about the frenetic three-day weekend. Certainly, San Francisco was a city-dweller's paradise. The performing arts, the museums, the food, the diversity. She'd never lack for entertainment. But she'd had all that and more in New York City. How many shows did she go to in the five years she'd lived there? Maybe three. And how often did she visit the Museum of Modern Art or the Whitney? Embarrassed to admit it even to herself, she only visited MOMA once, and she'd never gone to the Whitney Museum.

Driving down tree-lined Main Street, she slowed at the crowd standing outside Ruby's waiting for a table, as usual. And the Bistro Café's outside tables were full despite the heat. Sterling might roll up its sidewalks early during the week, but its citizens flocked to the antique stores, gift shops, boutiques, the bakery, and the restaurants on the weekends.

Her vision blurred as she came to the four-way stop on the corner of Main and First Street. *Damn.* A tear trickled down her cheek and into the corner of her mouth. When did she get so attached to this town? Was it the town, or was it Ethan? Or Delaney? Or maybe all of the above?

Thinking about pulling up even her shallow roots hurt far more than she'd ever expected.

Ethan glanced at the caller ID on his phone. His mom. Guilt poked at him. He'd been avoiding her.

"Mom."

"Ethan? I haven't heard from you. Are you okay?"

"Yeah, Mom. Sorry. I've just been busy."

"The new position?"

"Yeah." And sulking over Sam's breakup and impending departure.

"Why don't you and Sam come over for dinner on Friday? I'll make a big pot of beef stew."

He rubbed his hand over his face. He'd been hoping to avoid this topic, at least until the hole in his chest had mended. In which case he might never speak to his mother again. "Mom, I don't think Sam can make it."

"Oh, well, it doesn't have to be Friday."

He sighed. "Mom, Sam's likely leaving."

"What? Where's she going?"

"She's got a job offer out in California."

This revelation was met with silence.

"Mom?"

"Have you told her how you feel about her? That you love her?"

Love? Did he love Sam? Had it really happened that fast? He rubbed the ache behind his ribs. Yeah. It had happened that fast. "Mom—"

"I saw how you looked at her. And how she looked at you."

"Let's not go there. It's over."

"Maybe if you told her. Maybe she doesn't know—"

"Mom. It won't make a bit of difference. Listen, I'll come pick you up on Friday and take you to that restaurant in Carlyle, the one with the Bananas Foster."

"All right, sweetheart. I love you."

"Love you, too." He hung up the phone. *I love you.* Three little words that held so much meaning. And caused so much pain when they were left unspoken.

~

AFTER A FULL AND busy day on campus, Sam walked into her townhome. Guess there was no need to unpack those boxes in the dining room after all.

Kicking off her shoes, she set her purse, tote bag, and keys on the table in the foyer. Before she could even get a drink of water, her doorbell rang.

She opened the door to find Delaney standing there, hands on her hips, an annoyed expression on her face. "You were supposed to come by my office and tell me about your trip."

Sam opened the door wider, inviting Delaney in. "Sorry. It's been a rough day." She'd told her department chair about the job offer, which had gone over like a lead balloon. He'd been speechless, then cajoling, followed by a dose of annoyance. Guess she couldn't blame him. They'd gone to a great deal of trouble to bring her to Sterling.

Grabbing two diet sodas from the fridge, she handed one to Delaney. They settled in the living room, and Sam described her visit to San Francisco, the SoulMates.com campus in Silicon Valley, and the job offer, minus the salary and bonus numbers.

"I'm happy for you, if it's really what you want, but I can't believe you're leaving. You just got here." Delaney's blue eyes filled.

God, this was hard. Sam swallowed around the lump that had formed in her throat. "It's an offer I'd be crazy to refuse."

"I guess. But—"

Sam's phone rang. Her mother launched into her before she could say hello. "Is it true? Your dad just told me you're moving to San Francisco—"

Wincing, she interrupted, "Hi, Mom, how are you?"

"Don't be fresh with me," her mother reprimanded.

"Well, at least you're getting out of that backwater town. But industry? How can you sell out like that?"

Sell out! Sell out? This from a woman who'd made a small fortune on the bestselling couples self-help books she and her father had written.

"Mom, I have a friend over. Can I call you back?"

"A male friend?"

"Bye, Mom." Sam hung up the phone and tossed it onto the couch.

"And what about Ethan?" Delaney flung at her before she'd even recovered from her mother's barrage.

She was getting it from all sides today. "What about Ethan? What's he got to do with this?"

"How can you leave him like this when you're in love with him?"

"Love!" Sam threw up her hands with a mirthless laugh. "Where the hell did that come from?" Her heart beat a staccato against her ribs at the mention of love and Ethan in the same sentence.

"Really, Sam? And Denial is a river in Egypt."

"Denial? I'm not in denial."

Delaney snorted in disgust. "You've heard the phrase, 'physician, heal thyself'? How about 'psychologist, psycho-analyze thyself'? You're in total denial." Delaney rose, stalked over to Sam. "To the point that you're even denying your own research. Your own science."

Sam recoiled from the vehemence in Delaney's words.

"What are you so afraid of?"

That's the second time someone accused her of being afraid. "Nothing." Her voice sounded small. "I'm not afraid."

"You're running away from two people who love you." Delaney said, just above a whisper, as her eyes filled again.

"I'm not running—and Ethan doesn't love me."

"For someone who is supposed to be an expert in 'compatibility,'" she made air quotes around the word, "you don't know shit about love."

"And you do?" Sam threw back.

"Just because I haven't found Mr. Right doesn't mean I don't know how to love." Delaney grabbed her purse and tossed it over her shoulder heading for the door. "At least I don't run away every time things get difficult." Before walking out, she turned. "Just be damn sure this is what you want." She slammed the door so hard the windows rattled.

Stunned by her friend's violent departure, Sam sank back into the sofa. She'd been pissing off a lot of people lately. Why couldn't they see how important her career was to her?

Flopping back on the couch, she threw her arm over her eyes where tears threatened.

The doubts that had plagued her on the flight home returned.

When she'd decided to take the job at Sterling, there had been no doubts. She'd relished the opportunity the offer presented and looked forward to the challenge. This time, not so much. But if she were completely honest with herself, it wasn't just the job.

What are you so afraid of?

Were Ethan and Delaney right? Was she afraid?

Delaney had said she was running away from two people who love her. Did Ethan love her? Even more important, did she love Ethan? She missed him desperately. His laughter, his warmth, his sincerity. The way he made her feel, like she was the center of his universe. No one had ever made her feel so special.

And how had she repaid him? By accusing him of playing her, of disrespecting her and her work.

Wrapping her arms around herself, she buried her face in a pillow and cried. This pain and regret could only mean one thing—she was in love with Ethan Quinn.

EARLY THE FOLLOWING SATURDAY MORNING, Sam closed the lid on the last box. Looking around her now-empty lab, she breathed a sigh of relief. Done. The study was completed and she'd be moving next week. She laid the folder holding the final results on top of the box.

A lot had happened in the week since her visit to the SoulMates.com campus.

A few days after she'd told her department chair about the job offer, he'd called her into his office and offered her the moon to stay. Fast-track to tenure, an associate professor position immediately, more money, and even more importantly, a bigger lab.

She didn't tell him that she'd already made up her mind. About a lot of things.

Glancing at the results folder, she gnawed on her lip. She had several couples in the town and surrounding areas that she needed to inform, and she'd had another double-match. Jackie Ledbetter. One with Ethan, and another with Irwin Dumwilder, a nerdy physics professor, *a la* Sheldon Cooper. But there was one person she needed to give the results to first.

Setting the box on the moving cart, she picked up the folder and, flipping off the lights, headed for downtown Sterling. She had a parade to attend.

THE STERLING VOLUNTEER Fire Department threw candy to screaming kids from atop their fire truck, as Ethan walked along the parade route looking for a vantage point.

The Founder's Day Parade was in full swing by the time he got there. A blazing sun beat down on the parade-goers and turned ice cream cones into puddles of milk on the sidewalk.

Alone at the parade; this is not how Ethan had envisioned the day. He hadn't seen Sam at all, not even around campus. She was probably looking for a place to live in California.

He waved to Melanie and her husband then spotted Delaney standing on the corner, a ball cap pulled low over her eyes. He scanned the crowd thinking maybe Sam was with her, but there was no sign of her.

Give it up, man. She's moving on.

"Hi, Ethan!"

Gazing down, he saw Jackie Ledbetter's son. "Hi, Jack."

Where he was, his mom was sure to follow. A hand touched his arm from behind. "Why, Ethan! I wondered where you've been."

Yep. Jackie.

"Just been busy."

"I heard! A big congrats on the new job! Dean!"

"Interim," Ethan muttered.

The Sterling Equestrian Society cantered down Main Street.

"I can't see!" Jack hollered.

"Oh, Ethan, would you mind?" Jackie asked, her hand on his chest.

Ethan stepped back from her touch. "Sure." Leaning down, he lifted Jack onto his shoulders so he could see.

"Cool!" Jack said.

Jackie stepped closer, standing on tiptoes and leaning against Ethan for support. *Holy hell.*

"Isn't this fun?" Jackie giggled. "And maybe we can get some ice cream after the parade."

"Yeah!" Jack agreed.

"Sure." *Juuust shoot me.* No. This day was not turning out at all liked he'd planned.

SAM COULDN'T BELIEVE the crowd on Main Street. Ethan wasn't kidding when he'd said Founder's Day was a big deal. Red, white, and blue bunting decorated businesses, and the town's flag flew from the Victorian light posts lining the street.

The high school marching band played a Sousa march off key, while the cheerleaders waved their pompoms. Small Town, U.S.A.

Searching the crowd, she spotted a little boy, head and shoulders above everyone. The man who held him turned, and Sam's knees quivered. Ethan. And he was standing next to Jackie.

Jealousy, hot and sharp, knifed through her. Didn't take him long to get over her, she thought.

Feeling a little sick, she stopped and leaned against a light post. So much for her plan. She glanced down at the folder In her hand, tempted to toss it onto the overflowing trash can.

Turning, she headed back toward Ruby's. Her head hurt, and she could use some of Ruby's sweet iced tea.

With the parade in full swing, the diner only had a few patrons who'd given up on the heat and sought cooler climes. Taking a seat at the lunch counter, Sam dropped the folder onto the countertop and ordered her drink.

What did she expect? She'd broken up with Ethan. Of course he'd moved on. And with his other match. Made perfect sense.

That didn't make it any easier to take. She'd been such an idiot. She'd denied her own science, refusing to accept that Ethan was her histocompatible mate. But more than that—refusing to believe in love, when she'd clearly fallen helplessly in love with Ethan.

Taking a gulp of her iced tea, she relished the cool, soothing liquid. Then she pressed the glass to her cheek.

The bell over Ruby's door chimed, and someone sat in the empty seat next to her.

Turning, she gasped when she saw Ethan. Glancing behind him, she didn't see Jackie or her little boy.

"Hi," Ethan said.

"Hi," she breathed. God, how she'd missed him.

She slid the folder over to him. It's now or never. And he deserves to know.

"What's this?" Picking up the folder, he looked at her.

"Your results."

"My results from the love assay?"

She didn't bother to correct him this time. "Uh-huh."

"May I?"

"Of course. You said you wanted to know the results." She held her breath as he opened the file.

He stared at the paper with his two matches, saying nothing.

"You have . . ." She cleared her throat and continued, "You have two matches."

"Is that even possible?"

"It's not *impossible*, obviously."

Still nothing but a blank expression on his face. Well, she'd done what she needed to do. Throwing a five on the counter, she rose from her seat.

"Wait." He put his hand on her arm, and her skin tingled like she'd touched a live wire. "You mean to tell me you and I are a match?"

"And you and Jackie."

"And you've known you and I were a match since . . . when?"

Taking a deep breath, she replied, "Since July twenty-eighth." He still didn't mention his match to Jackie.

"You and Jackie are a match, too," she repeated. She would understand if he chose Jackie. *But it would still kill me.*

"Well, there would have been no contest." He waved his hand in the air as if it were a foregone conclusion.

No contest? What did that mean?

"You decide to give me this now, when you're leaving?" he continued, anger coloring his tone.

"You asked me what I was so afraid of." She blinked back tears. "Being wrong." She drew in a deep breath. "I was afraid of being wrong." A mirthless laugh escaped. "And, God, I've been wrong about so many things. And this job is just the latest."

"What other . . . things have you been wrong about, Dr. Love?" He set his hands on either side of her barstool, and her breath shallowed as his warm brown eyes searched hers.

"Relationships. Romance." She licked her dry lips. "Love."

"Love? Are you saying . . . ?"

"Yes. I'm saying I believe in romance now. And love."

He lifted a brow.

"My whole career I've denied the existence of love. That it's our chemistry, not our hearts, that determine who our best mates are. How could I admit that everything I'd built my professional life on was wrong?"

"Sam, your relationship theories and mine are not mutually exclusive."

"But, you said—"

"I know. I said I didn't agree with your theories. But what if we're both right? What if long, happy relationships are part chemistry, part romance? It's the chemistry that brings two people together. But it's the romance, along with mutual respect and love, that *keeps* them together."

His face blurred as her eyes filled. "I love you, Ethan."

"Did I just hear you say the 'L' word?" he asked, his voice incredulous.

"Do I need to say it again? I love you, Ethan, but I understand if you don't feel the same, especially after the way I've behaved . . . the things I've said." She held her breath, waiting.

His eyes softened, and his gaze moved to her mouth, then back up to her eyes, as his thumb captured the tear that rolled down her cheek. "I love you, too, Sam."

He loved her! She closed her eyes, and more tears spilled over.

"But, what about San Francisco?" Ethan asked, his voice rough with emotion.

"I turned them down. I'm not leaving."

"But—"

"I don't belong in industry. I belong in academia. I don't belong in San Francisco. I belong right here in Sterling." Closing her eyes, she drew in a deep breath, then opened them and looked into Ethan's warm brown eyes. "And according to our chemistry, I belong with you, if you'll still have me."

"Dr. Love, that's the most romantic thing you've ever said to me."

EPILOGUE

A month later, Sam walked into the main administration building for an appointment with the Provost, Dr. Chamberlain. Smoothing her skirt and adjusting the sleeves of her jacket, she gnawed on her lip. She and Ethan were finally being called on the carpet for their relationship.

Ethan's offer letter for the dean of the College of Arts and Sciences was on hold until the nepotism issue was resolved. She didn't want to leave Sterling, but she'd been secretly researching positions with universities in Atlanta and Athens. She could get an apartment and commute home to Sterling on the weekends. Not ideal, but she and Ethan could make it work if it meant the deanship he had worked so hard to achieve.

Drawing in a deep, calming breath, she approached the provost's receptionist. "I'm Dr. Love. I have a two o'clock meeting with Dr. Chamberlain."

"Right this way, Dr. Love."

She followed the young woman down the carpeted hallway and waited for her to announce her arrival to the provost. Sam halted in the doorway when she saw Ethan. How humiliating. The two of them called into the provost's office like two high-school kids called to the principal's office for kissing in the hallway. Ethan nervously wiped his hands on his pants.

Oh boy. Not good. Not good at all.

"Dr. Love," Dr. Chamberlain said, as he stepped forward. "Thank you for meeting with me today."

Like she had a choice. "My pleasure."

"Please, have a seat."

Unsure what to do—sit next to Ethan on the sofa or take a seat in the chair—she finally opted for the chair.

Ethan cast a confused glance at her, and she subtly shook her head.

"So," Dr. Chamberlain clapped his hands together, taking a seat across from them, "I understand the two of you are a couple."

Sam and Ethan answered together, "Yes."

"And Dr. Quinn is the final candidate for the dean of your college, if we can eliminate the nepotism issue. Otherwise . . ." Dr. Chamberlain shook his head, "we may need to hire the runner-up candidate."

Sam shot a look at Ethan, licked her dry lips, then spoke, "Dr. Chamberlain, I am prepared to—"

"If I may interrupt you," Dr. Chamberlain said, hand raised. "I believe I may have a solution."

Confused, she turned to Ethan. "The only solution I see is my departure from the university."

Ethan sprang to his feet. "No!"

"Now, Dr. Love, let's not be hasty. I think I have another possible solution. You see, we have two other couples in the university whose relationships raised similar issues. I convinced the university trustees that we could resolve the situation by permitting the reporting employee to report directly to me, thus bypassing the issue of reporting to his or her spouse."

Sam felt a glimmer of hope. Maybe she wouldn't have to leave Sterling.

"Of course," Dr. Chamberlain continued, "those couples were married, so there is a critical distinction between their circumstances and yours. I'm not sure I could persuade them to agree under the current circumstances," his voice trailed off.

"But if we were married," Ethan filled the silence, "that would solve the problem."

"Yes. I think it's safe to say that the trustees would accept the change in your reporting structure if you were married."

Coercing Ethan into marriage? No, this would not do. She would resign before she backed Ethan into that kind of corner.

Before she could speak her mind, Ethan walked over and took her hand. Dropping to one knee, he pulled a little turquoise box from his pocket and held it out to her.

Sam didn't know what to think. Pressing a shaking hand to her mouth, she looked over to see Dr. Chamberlain grinning from ear to ear. This had been a setup!

"Samantha, I've waited my whole life for you. Please say you'll be my wife so I can spend the rest of my life making you happy." Opening the box, he presented her with a brilliant pear-shaped diamond ring.

She laughed, and tears spilled down her cheeks. "How can I refuse my perfect histocompatible mate?"

ABOUT THE AUTHOR

Rebecca Heflin is an award-winning author who has dreamed of writing romantic fiction since she was fifteen and her older sister sneaked a copy of Kathleen Woodiwiss' Shanna to her and told her to read it.

Never quite sure what she wanted to be when she grew up, Rebecca didn't attend college until age 30, and earned her bachelor's in literature, before going on to complete her law degree.

Ever the late bloomer, Rebecca finally turned her attention to fulfilling her dream of writing, and published her first novel at age 48. When not passionately pursuing her dream, Rebecca is busy with her day-job at a major state university.

She and her husband are also co-founders of a non-profit organization, which raises money to help cancer patients and their families.

Rebecca's pen name is an abbreviated version of her great-great grandmother's name: Sarah Anne Rebecca Heflin Apple Smith. Whew! And you wonder why she shortened it.

Rebecca and her mountain-climbing husband live in central Virginia.

<u>Sign up</u> for Rebecca's newsletter for all the latest news on upcoming releases, appearances, and contests.

Catch up with Rebecca on the web
www.rebeccaheflin.com

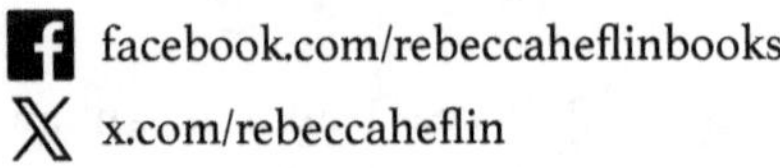 facebook.com/rebeccaheflinbooks
x.com/rebeccaheflin

ALSO BY REBECCA HEFLIN:

THE PROMISE OF CHANGE

RESCUING LACEY

DREAMS COME TRUE SERIES

DREAMS OF PERFECTION, BOOK 1

SHIP OF DREAMS, BOOK 2

DREAMS OF HER OWN, BOOK 3

STERLING UNIVERSITY SERIES

WINNING DR. WENTWORTH, BOOK 2

EDUCATING DR. MAYFIELD, BOOK 3

SEASONS OF NORTHRIDGE SERIES

A SEASON TO DANCE, BOOK 1

A SEASON TO LOVE, BOOK 2

A SEASON TO REMEMBER, BOOK 3

A SEASON TO GIVE, BOOK 4

WHIRLWIND ROMANCE

UNDER THE PARIS MOON, BOOK 1